The Curse of the
Viking Grave

FARLEY MOWAT

The Curse of the Viking Grave

ILLUSTRATED BY CHARLES GEER

McClelland and Stewart

The Canadian Publishers
McClelland and Stewart Limited
25 Hollinger Road, Toronto

Manufactured in Canada by Webcom Limited

For my sons
ROBERT ALEXANDER MOWAT
and
PETER DAVID MOWAT,
with love

Books by Farley Mowat

People of the Deer
The Regiment
The Dog Who Wouldn't Be
The Grey Seas Under
The Desperate People
The Serpent's Coil
Never Cry Wolf
Westviking
Canada North
This Rock Within the Sea
   (with John de Visser)
The Boat Who Wouldn't Float
Sibir
A Whale for the Killing
Wake of the Great Sealers (with David Blackwood)

FOR YOUNG READERS
Owls in the Family
Lost in the Barrens
The Black Joke
The Curse of the Viking Grave

EDITED BY FARLEY MOWAT
Coppermine Journey
The Top of the World trilogy
Ordeal by Ice
The Polar Passion
Tundra

Contents

The Curse of the
Viking Grave

CHAPTER 1

Schoolroom in the Bush

On the windswept ice of a lake in northern Manitoba two ravens sat hunched beside the frozen carcass of a caribou. Foxes and wolves had left precious little meat on the bones of the dead animal and the ravens circled each other threateningly while the sound of their harsh, disputing voices echoed across the subarctic silence of the lake.

Shambling through the dark woods along the shore, a wolverine raised his heavy head and listened. The cries of the ravens told him there was food nearby, and so he swung purposefully out on the ice in the direction of the birds.

On the north shore of the lake, where a clump of spruce trees stood thick and tall, a white husky sniffed the frigid air. He caught the musky taint of wolverine and his hackles rose. Throwing back his head he howled a challenge down the lake. At once a dozen other huskies sprang to their feet and joined in the wailing chorus.

Nestled snugly amongst the protecting trees near where the dogs were tethered stood a long, low cabin whose two windows stared owlishly out over Macnair Lake. Inside

this cabin Angus Macnair put down a book he had been reading aloud and stepped to the nearest window. He watched the dogs intently for a moment or two, then, with a shake of his red, piratical beard, he turned to face three boys who were watching him expectantly.

"Nay, lads. 'Tisna caribou they dogs is howlin' after. Wolves maybe . . . or a wolverine. But dinna fuss yer-sel's, they caribou wull soon be comin' back this way and then we'll hae fresh meat again."

He settled himself into a chair, picked up the book and continued with the lesson for the day.

Angus Macnair hardly looked the part of a school-teacher. He was a massive and craggy-faced trapper who had lived in the Canadian northlands since leaving the

Orkney Islands at the age of thirteen. The schoolroom
was the Macnair cabin, a cluttered and low-ceilinged log
structure redolent with the gamey smell from scores of
pelts that hung drying from the rafters. Here Angus
taught school for three days each week. During the re-
mainder of the week teacher and students were absent
from Macnair Lake, tending their traplines which ran for
as much as fifty miles to the north, east, west and south.

As Angus continued reading, his nephew Jamie listened
from his perch on a log beside the sheet-iron stove. Jamie's
blue-eyed, sharp-featured face, under a mat of unkempt
blond hair, was bent over a wooden stretcher balanced on
his knees, as with practiced hand he scraped the flesh side
of a fox skin with a blunt knife blade.

Next to him, on the edge of a log bunk, sat Awasin Mee-wasin, the son of the chief of the Cree Indians who lived at nearby Thanout Lake. Awasin was lean and dark, black-eyed and black-haired, and as taut and wiry as a rabbit snare.

The third "student" was by all odds the most striking member of the trio. His amiable, high-cheekboned face would have seemed Oriental had it not been for his wide blue eyes and the tangle of flaming red hair hanging over his forehead. This was Peetyuk. His father had been a wandering English trapper named Frank Anderson. Many years earlier Anderson had gone far out into the open Barrens to the north of Macnair Lake to spend a winter trapping white fox. Here he had met and married an Eskimo woman. Shortly before the birth of his child, Anderson had gone through the spring ice of a lake and had been drowned, leaving his son Peetyuk to be raised by the Eskimos.

The boys were particularly interested in the book Angus was reading them this day. It was a history of the early Norwegian voyages to America made long before the time of Columbus. The chapter Angus had begun that morning described how, about the year 1360, a Viking expedition sailed to Greenland and then on to North America, perhaps by way of Hudson Bay. Then it told of the finding of a strangely inscribed stone at Kensington, Minnesota, in 1898. This stone bore a message in Runic, the ancient writing of the Nordic peoples.

"When the inscription was translated," Angus continued, "it proved to be a record left by eight Swedes and twenty Norwegians on an exploring journey to the west. The runes told how the party camped one night on an island in a lake. The next day most of them went fishing, leaving ten men to guard the camp. When the fishermen returned they found their comrades dead and covered with blood. The runes also spoke of an additional ten men who had been left to guard the expedition's ship at a place on the sea fourteen days' distance from the scene of the massacre. The date carved on the stone was 1362 . . ."

Angus looked up. "Here's a picture of yon stane, wi' all its markin's," he told the boys. "Aye, Jamie and they look verra like the markin's on the wee bit o' lead Jamie and Awasin found awa out on the Barrens last summer. Fetch it to me, Jamie, and we'll hae a look."

Jamie jumped to his feet and from a shelf under the rafters brought down a piece of sheet lead about six inches square. The boys clustered around Angus as the trapper laid the little lead plaque on the page opposite the drawing of the Kensington Stone.

"Nae doot about it! The markin's are the same sort. I wouldna wonder if the cache where ye found yon bit of lead was made by the self-same lot what carved yon stane. Och! 'Tis too bad we canna read the writin', laddies."

Jamie's eyes shone with excitement. "If the writing *is* the same, then the other stuff we saw at that cache must be Norse too. I'll bet it's worth a fortune!"

"A fortune? Aye. But if they things ye found are truly Norse they're worth a guid deal mair than money, lad. 'Twould maybe help to write a whole new chapter in the history of America. In any case we'll surely make a trip out to yon place come summertime — though wi' considerable more care than you two took."

Jamie and Awasin had the grace to look shame-faced. They were remembering only too vividly their nearly fatal journey of the previous year when they accompanied a Chipeweyan hunting party on a visit to the Barrenlands and discovered the mysterious cache. Through their own willfulness they became separated from the Indians, lost their canoe and most of their gear on a rapid, and were then forced to spend several months struggling desperately to survive the Barrenlands winter. In the end they escaped with their lives only because they were lucky enough to encounter Peetyuk and the Eskimos.*

Angus closed the book and put it carefully on a shelf with the score or so of well-worn volumes which formed his treasured library.

"School's over for the week," he told the boys. "Awa' wi' ye the noo and do yere chores while I cook up a meal."

When the boys had gone outside Angus stood at the window for a minute and watched them fondly. Peetyuk was busy chopping birch logs into stove lengths while Jamie and Awasin took turns wielding a long ice-chisel to open a water hole in the frozen lake. As Angus watched he pondered on the circumstances which had brought these three to his once lonely cabin.

Jamie had come to him from a southern Canadian city three years earlier when he lost both his parents in an au-

---

* The story of this adventure is told in Farley Mowat's *Lost in the Barrens.*

tomobile accident, leaving Angus as his only living rela-
tive. During those years Jamie had changed from a rather
puny boy to a tough and competent youth who was now
almost as much at home in the subarctic forests as was
Awasin, who had been born there.

The farthest south Awasin had ever been was to the
mission school at Pelican Narrows (a mere two hundred
miles away), where he had learned to speak and read
good English. But Awasin hungered after knowledge, and
when Angus Macnair began schooling Jamie, Awasin easily persuaded his father, Alphonse Meewasin, to let him
spend the winter months at the Macnair cabin as one of
Angus's students.

Peetyuk came to join the little group at Macnair Lake as
a result of his accidental meeting with Jamie and Awasin
in the Barrenlands. The Eskimo band to which Peetyuk's
mother belonged brought the two rescued boys south to
safety. When the Eskimos returned to their own country
they left Peetyuk in Angus Macnair's care since they believed it was time for the boy to learn something of the
world of his dead father, Frank Anderson.

By the time the woodbox and the water pails were full
Angus had lunch ready. It consisted of a savory mess of
barley boiled up with dried caribou meat and a slab of fat
pork. Big chunks of fresh sourdough bread and pint mugs
of sweet black tea went with it.

The boys lingered long over the meal, discussing plans
for a summer expedition to the Barrens to revisit the

strange stone cache. They might have spent the whole of the short winter afternoon talking about the projected trip if Angus had not recalled them to reality.

"Och, laddies! This is no way to make a catch of fur. Awa' wi' ye noo! And see to it ye bring hame a fine load o' pelts. We'll be wantin' the money to pay for new canoes and a' the other gear we'll be needin' for yon trip tae Eskimo Land."

Setting the example himself, Angus pulled on his big parka, his deerskin mittens and his heavy moccasins. When he shouldered his pack and started for the door, the boys were close behind him.

In his hurry to be the first away Jamie sprinted to his cariole (the narrow toboggan which bush trappers favor), where he dumped his pack before springing to the dog-line to unleash his huskies. He had three dogs. Two were small, rangy beasts which had belonged to his uncle. The third was a huge white husky called Fang — one of two lost Eskimo dogs Awasin and Jamie had found out on the Barrens.

The yard now became a pandemonium of shouting boys and howling dogs. Peetyuk was the first to get his team harnessed, and with a derisive shout of farewell he jumped on the tail end of his long Eskimo sled and went careening off to the southward over the lake ice. Jamie and Awasin got away a few moments later. For a while their teams ran neck and neck, each straining to draw ahead of the other. But when Jamie began shouting "Chaw! Chaw!" his team obediently turned left, swinging toward the eastern side of the lake.

Angus was still methodically hitching up his dogs as the two carioles and the sled raced away from the cabin. He shook his head as he watched the wild progress of the three boys, but he was smiling.

"Juliet, lass," he said as he tightened his lead dog's belly strap, "they're a' three of them as daft as badgers."

Juliet whined in reply, then thrust her shoulders against the traces, giving the signal to the other dogs to take a strain. Sedately she led the team out onto the ice and Angus's cariole turned away on the long northern trail.

The chill silence of a January afternoon settled down over the cabin as a last fugitive wisp of blue smoke curled upward through the old black chimney pipe.

CHAPTER 2

The Chill That Kills

ONLY THE HARSH CHATTERING OF Canada jays scavenging in the refuse pile broke the silence at the cabin during the next four days while Angus and the boys were away on their traplines. Not until early afternoon of the fourth day did smoke begin to rise again in a blue haze from the chimney. Awasin's cariole stood upended in freshly fallen snow beside the cabin door while his dogs, weary after a final run of thirty miles through the soft snow in the forests, lolled panting in front of their little log hutches. Awasin had driven them hard in order to be first home. But he barely had the kettle boiling when Jamie's team came dashing up the gentle slope from the lake shore.

"What kept you so long?" Awasin asked insultingly.

Jamie made no reply. Whistling to himself he tied his leader to a tree, then he picked up a big, dark object from his cariole. He walked up to the cabin and casually dropped it at Awasin's feet.

The Indian boy crouched down to stare incredulously. "A fisher!" he cried admiringly as he stroked the beautiful dark fur. "Only once before have I seen such a one. Where did you catch it, Jamie?"

"In a marten trap in the spruce woods beyond my second overnight cabin," Jamie replied. "Probably lots more of them around, only it takes a real trapper to get them."

Awasin was too impressed to rise to the bait. The fisher is one of the rarest and most valuable of all woodland mammals. Awasin carried it reverently into the cabin and laid it on the table where he could examine it in detail from its sharp, weasel face to the magnificent bushy tail.

He was interrupted by the renewed howling of dogs. This time they were announcing Peetyuk's arrival. Just at dusk Angus Macnair also reached home.

It had been a good trip all around. Peetyuk had two foxes, a marten, three ermine weasels and a mink. Awasin had two mink and two red foxes. Angus, whose trapline was the longest of all, had three foxes, two mink, a weasel and an otter. Jamie had caught only one red fox in addition to the fisher, but the fisher alone was worth nearly the total catch of the other trappers.

After supper kerosene lanterns were lit and everyone got down to work. As they skinned, cleaned and stretched the pelts they discussed their small adventures. Awasin told of putting his leg through a thin spot in the ice while setting an otter trap, and of having to light a fire and dry his moccasin before his foot froze solid. Jamie reported that a wolverine had broken into one of his overnight cabins and had eaten all his grub so that he had to make do with ptarmigan which he shot with his .22 rifle. Peetyuk had encountered two Chipeweyan Indians bound south for the trading post at Reindeer Lake from the Chipeweyan winter camps at timber line on Kasmere Lake. But it was Angus's news that roused the most interest. At the extreme north end of his line he had seen fresh signs of deer.

Following the pattern of their annual migration, the caribou had come south out of the Barrens early in the autumn, seeking shelter in the forests. But the main herds had swept past Macnair Lake in a matter of a week, then had swung westward and disappeared. From what Angus was reporting now, it appeared that they had circled north and east and were drifting south once more. The return of the deer was a prospect which excited everyone, since apart from rabbits and ptarmigan there had been no fresh meat at Macnair Lake for three long months.

When talk of the caribou died down Angus returned to

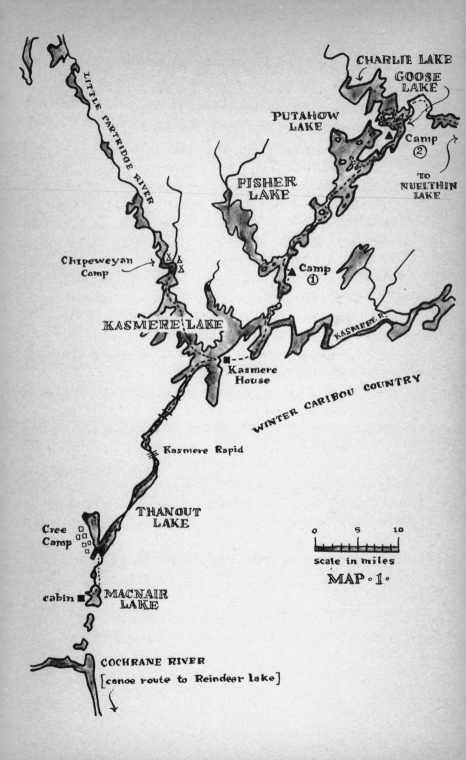

LITTLE PARTRIDGE RIVER

CHARLIE LAKE

GOOSE LAKE

PUTAHOW LAKE

FISHER LAKE

Camp ②

TO NUELTHIN LAKE

Camp ①

Chipeweyan Camp

KASMERE LAKE

KASMERE R.

Kasmere House

WINTER CARIBOU COUNTRY

Kasmere Rapid

THANOUT LAKE

Cree Camp

0   5   10

scale in miles

MAP · 1 ·

cabin   MACNAIR LAKE

COCHRANE RIVER

[canoe route to Reindeer lake]

Peetyuk's meeting with the Chipeweyans — the Idthen Eldeli, or Deer Eaters, as they called themselves.

"'Tis a strange time o' the year for they fellows to be traveling south," he mused. "Did they no say why they were awa', Peetyuk?"

Peetyuk shook his head. "I not able speak their tongue. But they look hungry, and they go in big hurry. They carry no furs on sleds, and dogs look starved."

"They're a strange lot, they Chips," Angus mused. "They try to live as their ancestors did a century ago, but that canna be done nae mair. Last year they nigh starved to death and maybe they have more trouble the noo. Ah weel, Alphonse Meewasin will ken. I stopped by to see him at Thanout Lake the day, but he was awa' on his trapline. Your mither says he'll be doon for a visit soon, Awasin, to see how your schoolin' goes, nae doot."

Alphonse Meewasin came sooner than expected. At lunchtime the next day the dogs announced the arrival of a visitor, and a few minutes later the tall, gaunt form of the Cree chief stood in the doorway. Under his arm was a small parcel done up in deer hide, and with a barely suppressed smile on his lips he held out the parcel to Peetyuk.

"It must be that my daughter Angeline does not think the Ayuskeemo* can make good boots," he explained. "And so she sends you these . . ."

The parcel contained two pairs of beautifully worked moosehide moccasins, elaborately decorated with red,

* "Eskimo" is our version of the Cree word Ayuskeemo.

green and gold beadwork. Peetyuk stood holding them in his hands, much embarrassed, and uncertain what to do or say.

"Now you're in trouble, Pete!" Jamie cried joyfully. "When a Cree girl makes moccasins for a fellow . . . that's the end of him. Isn't that right, Awasin?"

Awasin nodded his head solemnly. "That is so. And my sister has never made moccasins for any man before. I must watch you close, Peetyuk. I am her brother, do not forget!"

Peetyuk, his face almost as red as his hair, turned in dismay to Awasin, who stared sternly back at him. "But *I* do nothing," he cried. "Not speak her at all, even."

Peetyuk's torment was cut short by Alphonse, who turned to address Angus. "Yesterday morning I passed close to the Idthen Eldeli camp at Kasmere Lake and the women were wailing the death songs. Before I could go to the tents I was stopped by the old chief, Denikazi. He said there was a great sickness in the camp, and already some had died. All were sick except himself and some old people and the hunters Penyatzi and Madees, and these two he had sent south to seek aid from the white men."

Angus's face clouded.

" 'Tis bad news you bring, Alphonse. Do ye ken what ails them?"

"Only that it is a lung sickness. It brings the burning fevers and then the chill that kills."

"Then there's little doot about it," Angus muttered half to himself. " 'Tis influenza, certain sure. They would have brought it back wi' them from the Christmas visit to the mission." He looked up and asked sharply. "How are your ane people, Alphonse? Any sickness amongst them?"

Alphonse shook his head. "We are well. And I have sent two sledloads of whitefish to Denikazi's camp so that his people will not starve."

Angus placed his hand on his friend's shoulder. "Aye," he said, "ye would do all ye can to help. But hark now. Your people must have nae mair contact with they Chips. I'll see to it they get food. Influenza does na' strike white men as it does the Indians. And I have some good news. The deer are coming south. Me and the lads wull give over trapping for the time being and wi' a few of your men to help, we'll hunt meat for Denikazi's band."

Alphonse's news brought about a drastic change in the boys' lives. Schooling stopped entirely and so did trapping. The following morning they set out for the country north and east of Thanout Lake where Angus had encountered the deer, leaving Angus to make the round of their traplines and spring all the traps. They had orders to travel hard until they were well into the herds and to kill all the deer they could in two days' hunting. Then they were to cache what they could not carry and head for the Idthen Eldeli camps with fully laden carioles. Angus was to meet them near the sickness camp and deliver the meat to Denikazi's people.

The boys encountered the first deer on the south shores of Kasmere Lake but, mindful of their instructions, they continued northeast down the Kasmere River until they were in the midst of the drifting herds.

They quickly made camp and for two days hunted caribou which congregated on the myriad little lakes of the district. Two of the boys would hide with rifles ready while the third drove his team out onto the ice and panicked the deer into headlong flight toward the ambush.

By the end of the second day some twenty deer had been killed and readied for carrying. The following morning the boys set out for the Idthen Eldeli camps, driving their laden sleds up the Kasmere River onto the broad ice of Kasmere Lake. Along its northern arm they came in sight of a few thin coils of smoke from Chipeweyan teepees which stood in the scrubby bush beside the mouth of the Kasba River.

They were met far out on the lake ice by Angus, who had been impatiently watching for them. He helped them cache their loads on a tiny islet from which he could ferry the meat to the camps of the sick and starving Chipeweyans.

"Hurry now, lads," Angus ordered. "Ye must get back here wi' another load by tomorrow for I've decided I must gang south myself. They traders and missionaries will pay little heed to what Penyatzi and Madees tell them but it may be they'll listen to me. If they canna, or willna help, then I'll hie on south to The Pas and report to the authorities. They Chips must have doctors and medicine. They're in a terrible bad way, and if we dinna stop this epidemic it may sweep the whole country. Hearken now! When I'm gone ye're to dump your loads on the ice half a mile awa' from the camp. There's one or two Chips still able to get around, and they must come for the meat. Ye're not to go nigh the tents. But if it should come on so bad for they puir people that ye *must* go to their camp, Jamie wull be the one to go. Alone! Ye understand?"

Some two days later, Angus had ferried the last load of meat to the Chipeweyan camp. He said good-by to the boys and started the long trip — almost two hundred miles — to the nearest trading post. And he might have to travel another hundred and fifty miles to reach the first real settlement, at The Pas.

Throughout the rest of that month and into the first week of February the three boys, assisted by some of Alphonse's Cree hunters, labored to help the stricken Chipeweyans. Load after load of meat was brought in by the hunters, while others of the Crees freighted firewood to the death camp.

But food and wood were not enough. The people of the Idthen Eldeli camp were so sick that most of them could no longer help themselves even to the extent of lighting fires or cooking food. Chief Denikazi himself was struck down, and though he could still crawl from his tent to hack off raw chunks of frozen meat, he too was fast growing weaker. Each time the boys came within sight of the huddle of pointed skin tents they saw fewer and fewer signs of life.

By the end of the first week in February they could stand it no longer. They made their decision, and that night in Alphonse Meewasin's cabin at Thanout Lake they announced it. They were young, they argued to Alphonse, and in good health. They believed they could survive the disease even if they caught it. They were determined to move into the Chipeweyan camp and to do what they could to nurse the dying Indians. Awasin and Peetyuk would not allow Jamie to tackle the job single-handed. There was logic on their side, for one boy could not have coped alone.

Alphonse and Marie Meewasin gave their permission, but with a terrible reluctance.

"We will bring meat and wood each day," Alphonse told them. "May the spirits hold your lives firmly in their hands, my sons."

The squalor and misery of the Chipeweyan camps was incredible. For weeks no one there had had the strength to clean out the tents, or even to remove the dead. Moving from tent to tent, the three boys drew on one another for the strength to continue with their appalling task. Their faces hardened at the things they saw, and their stomachs turned over — yet they did not weaken in their resolve. The Chipeweyans had been their friends, and in the north there is nothing one will not do to help a friend.

Soon they were having some measure of success in their battle against the disease. Roaring fires and the strength of steaming meat soup brought renewed life to those Chipeweyans who had suffered the ravages of the disease and survived it. By the end of a week more than a score of men and women had passed the crisis and had rallied back to life — but an almost equal number had lost the struggle.

The boys got very little rest. All through the long winter

nights two boys made continual rounds of the tents to keep the fires going, while the third stretched out in exhausted sleep. They thought of only one thing: when would help come? Each day they strained their eyes across the lake to glimpse the approach of Alphonse's men, hoping that Angus Macnair and a doctor might be with them.

On a day in the last week of February, Alphonse brought a load of food to the meeting place and was met only by Jamie. The boy stood thirty yards away, as had been agreed, and he was so weary that he seemed to sag into the snow.

Alphonse's face betrayed his fear, but he spoke calmly enough.

"Where are the others?" he asked.

"It's Peetyuk," Jamie answered. "He's sick, and Awasin's staying in the camp with him. Awasin's all right and so am I. When is help coming, Alphonse? Is there no word from my uncle yet?"

Alphonse's dark and handsome face grew darker still. He stretched out his hands as if he would close the gap between himself and the boy.

"You have much strength in you, Jamie," he said. "Be strong now, for the news is bad."

"Angus!" Jamie shouted. "Is he all right? Did he get through?"

"He did what he said he would, my son. Last night a messenger came from The Pas, a Cree sent by the police. He brought a letter to you from the police — but also he brought private news.

"When Angus reached Reindeer he found Penyatzi and Madees lying in a travel tent some distance from the trading post. They were very sick and none would go near them. So your uncle nursed Penyatzi and Madees. Madees still lives, although Penyatzi is no more.

"There was no help available at the trading post, so Angus traveled on. But he took the evil with him in his lungs. He got to The Pas sick. He was taken to the hospital and for a time they thought he would die. But he lives, my son, he lives. And he has sent this message to you through the lips of his friends the Crees. He says this: 'Tell the boy he is to do as he sees fit, for he has shown himself to be a man, and a man may decide his own life for himself.' "

Alphonse finished talking and laid a manila envelope on the snow. As he walked away from it, Jamie ran forward, picked it up and tore it open.

The Pas, Manitoba
February 18th

Jamie Macnair
Macnair Lake
Manitoba

Dear Sir:

Re: Angus Macnair

1.   I have to inform you that your uncle, Angus Macnair, is hospitalized at The Pas with double pneumonia and serious complications. It is the opinion of the doctors that he will not be able to leave his bed for many

weeks and he will be unable to return north for some months, if ever.

2.   Since he has no funds he is being cared for as a welfare patient.

3.   It is understood that Mr. Macnair is your legal guardian. Since he is not in a position to care for you the law compels me to instruct you to report yourself to the Child Welfare authorities in Winnipeg as soon as possible.

4.   You will therefore return to The Pas with the bearer of this letter, Special Constable Peter Moiestie. Transportation by rail to Winnipeg will be provided for you from there.

5.   Would you please inform Chief Denikazi and Chief Meewasin that the Department of Indian Affairs has the epidemic under advisement and will try to arrange a visit by a doctor when conditions warrant.

ROBERT OWEN, Sgt.,
i/c The Pas Detachment

CHAPTER 3
Angeline

Shock and rage choked Jamie as he finished the letter. He looked up, white-faced and hard-eyed.

"Listen to this, Alphonse!" he cried bitterly, and read the letter aloud.

There was a responsive anger on the Cree chief's face. "So," he said, "they will send a doctor — when conditions warrant! Then we will show him many graves. But you, my son, what will you do?"

"I'm staying!" Jamie yelled fiercely. "You can tell Constable Moiestie if he wants me he'll find me in Denikazi's tent — with five sick Chips. He can come in there and get me if he wants to try it."

"Easy, my son. Peter Moiestie is a Cree. Have no fear of him. He will return south without you if that is what you wish. But you must think carefully of what you do, for it is in my mind that the police will send for you again."

"There's plenty of other things to think about," Jamie replied more calmly. "There's Angus being treated like a down-and-out. I've got to get money to take care of him — maybe for a long time. I can't do that in an orphanage and that's likely where they'll put me if I go outside. But if I stay here I can go on trapping and, and . . . there's the Viking relics! They're bound to be worth a lot of money. And we can still go north for them! That's it, Alphonse, that'll solve everything!"

Alphonse stepped nearer and nodded his head thoughtfully. "Perhaps you are right, my son. But you must remember that you are a white man, and the whites will not let you go so easily. Do not forget that they are your people."

Jamie clenched his hands, wadded the letter into a ball and flung it onto the ice. There was bitter defiance in his voice.

"*My* people? They aren't mine! They'd let the whole lot of you die without lifting a hand to help. Don't call them *my* people, Alphonse!"

Adroitly Alphonse changed the subject.

"The decision is yours to make," he said soothingly. "Your uncle left you free to do as you think best. But now, if the Idthen Eldeli can spare you, it would be wise to bring Peetyuk back to your cabin where he can be better cared for."

Mention of Peetyuk quieted Jamie's anger. "I guess you're right, Alphonse. The Chips can get along without us now, so long as you keep bringing them wood and meat. And Peetyuk *is* pretty sick."

The next morning as Jamie and Awasin harnessed the dogs to the carioles, Chief Denikazi appeared from his tent, still weak but holding himself stiffly upright in the cold wind. He said nothing until Peetyuk, who was half delirious with fever, had been carefully placed in Awasin's cariole and well wrapped in deerskins. Then he grunted to attract the boys' attention and, without even looking at them, muttered a few words.

"What's he saying?" asked Jamie, who did not understand Chipeweyan.

"He says: 'We will be here,'" Awasin translated.

"Well, *that's* not much of a thank-you speech, considering all we've done."

Awasin glanced sharply at his friend and his usually gentle voice had an edge to it.

"Sometimes I think you do not know us at all, Jamie. What use is a speech made out of many words? Denikazi means that as long as there are Chipeweyans in this land, we will have friends. Is that not enough?"

Jamie fumbled with one of the traces and muttered: "I'm sorry, Awasin. Tell him we were glad to help his people."

"There is no need, Jamie. He knows. Now let us go."

A few minutes later, the boys looked back to see the old Chipeweyan still watching them. He grew small in the distance before he turned his back. Slowly Denikazi walked toward the straggling row of deerskin tents. Many of them now stood empty to the winds, while the people who had built them waited in rigid silence under the great snowdrifts — waited for spring and the thawing of the ground so that they could begin the long sleep of the dead.

The boys made the homeward journey at a good pace, for the two teams had been strengthened by the addition of Peetyuk's dogs. Because of the danger of infecting the Crees they swung wide around the camps at Thanout Lake, but as they passed the cabins most of the Crees came out to wave and shout greetings to them from a distance. Just after dark the carioles swung down Macnair Lake.

Jamie and Awasin had expected to find a deserted cabin, frosty cold after the long weeks it had stood empty. They were startled to see a soft gleam of yellow light from the two windows. They looked quickly to see if there were a sled and dogs in the yard, but there was nothing. It was all very mysterious, for it had been agreed that they should have no contact with the Crees until Peetyuk was completely over his sickness. And yet, who else but one of the Crees could have visited the cabin?

They had not long to wait for an answer. As the dogs hauled the carioles up off the lake ice they broke into a short chorus of howls, and the cabin door swung open. Framed in the lighted space was the figure of a girl. She held a kerosene lantern in her hand and it illuminated her pretty oval face and reflected the gleam of her long, black hair.

"Angeline!" Awasin cried in amazement. "What are you doing here? You must leave at once! We have Peetyuk with us and he has the lung sickness. We must get him inside. Pick up your things and go!"

"Bring him in then, quickly," the girl replied calmly. "The cabin is ready. There is hot soup on the stove. And

do not tell me what *I* must do, brother, for our mother has permitted me to come, and our father has brought me here himself. Hurry with Peetyuk. Do not stand there like two frozen owls."

Too astonished to argue, the boys did as they were told. Not until some time later, when the sick boy had been freshly clothed, put into his bunk, fed a little soup and had drowsed off into a feverish sleep, did they have time to question Angeline. The girl, who was busy washing dishes and setting pots of water to boil, was perfectly aware that she had them at a disadvantage. It was not until Awasin finally abandoned his big-brother attitude and pleaded with her for an explanation that she turned, smiling, and told her story.

"You have forgotten, brother, that when I was at mission school as a little girl there was the lung sickness there. I had it, but it did me no harm. When our father told us that you were coming here with Peetyuk I spoke of the need for someone to care for him, and our mother understood. Father agreed, and he brought me here this mornning. It is a good thing I came. Look at you two! A bear would turn you out of his cave, you smell so bad! Here is hot water, and here clean clothing. Unless you would sleep outside with the dogs tonight, make yourselves clean!"

There is no false modesty amongst northern peoples, and Awasin bowed to the inevitable meekly enough. In a moment he had stripped off his filthy clothing and was washing himself in a bucket of scalding water, sighing with pleasure as he did so.

But being city-raised, Jamie found the situation more difficult. Finally he picked up a bucket and went out to the unheated lean-to shed at the back of the cabin where they stored things which would not be hurt by frost. Nobody said anything to him as he went out into the bitter cold, but as he stood shivering in the shed with the hot water sending up a great cloud of steam about him, he distinctly heard the sound of giggling from the cabin, and despite himself he blushed.

"Darn girl," he complained to himself, careful to keep his voice low. "She's got no business here!"

But an hour later as he lay back on his bunk, clean and freshly clothed in a shirt and trousers Angeline had laundered that afternoon, he found that his indignation had mellowed considerably. He was even able to thank Angeline in a moderately friendly manner when she brought him a mug of coffee and asked for his moccasins so that she could mend their worn-out soles.

Peetyuk was indeed very ill and the long trip in the cariole had done him no good. It was several days before the fever left him. During those days Angeline cared for him with deep solicitude. She was merciless with Jamie and Awasin. Although she fed them well and saw to it that their ragged trail clothes were neatly repaired, she drove them to tasks they would normally not have bothered with. She made them scrub the grimy cabin from end to end. She forced Jamie to spend a whole day making more shelves where clothing and other oddments of gear, which had lain helter-skelter anywhere, could be stowed neatly away. She sent Awasin off to snare snowshoe rabbits which, she said, made the best soup for sick people.

Despite the way she took control, she never raised her voice and never appeared to be giving orders. She was always demure, soft-spoken, smiling — and utterly inflexible. Jamie was baffled by her. Most of the time he resented her presence, but when he chose to be honest with himself he was grateful for the way she cared for Peetyuk and so eased the burden which would otherwise have fallen on himself and Awasin.

Although Angeline made the boys do what she required, she also saw to it that they had a chance to rest and regain their strength after the ordeal at the Chipeweyan camp. Cooking and nursing were nothing new to her for she had done both of these at home and at the mission school. But it was almost as if the Macnair cabin had become her own house and she felt a tremendous (if carefully concealed) pleasure in seeing to the domestic details. Nor was she unaware that Peetyuk, growing stronger every day, watched her busy activities with open admiration.

Awasin was resigned to her presence almost from the first. He knew his sister, and he had no intention of wasting time and energy pitting his will against hers. Besides, he recognized her value and was secretly delighted to have the benefits of her presence.

One day about a week after their return Awasin and Jamie were cutting wood together and talking about the fix Angus was in, and of what they could do about it.

"Peetyuk is much better now," Awasin said. "With Angeline to keep the cabin and look after him, perhaps we
should start trapping again. Long-hair fur is still prime
and the time is coming for the muskrat and beaver. Soon
my father will go south to the trading post to clear his
winter debt and to outfit for the spring hunt. We can send
our furs with him and he can buy the things we will need
when we go north to the Barrenlands."

Jamie brightened visibly at this suggestion. He had
been doing much brooding about his problems, and the
worry of being responsible for finding money to free his
uncle from the degradation of being treated as a welfare
case was weighing heavily on him.

"You're right, Awasin. We ought to go back to trapping.
You and I can take our old lines and split up Peetyuk's
between us until he's well enough to travel. Maybe we can
even run part of Angus's line as well. With the furs we've
already got and what we can get before break-up, we
ought to be able to ship a good few bales south. We'll send
the best of them straight to The Pas. There's a fur buyer
there Angus knows and trusts, and he'll sell them and see
to it Angus gets some money."

So it was decided, and the next morning the two boys
said good-by to a wan Peetyuk who still lay in his bunk.

Angeline helped pack their carioles and saw them off.
When they made their first stop for lunch they found she
had filled their grub-boxes with frozen doughnuts, packages of frozen caribou stew, and loaves of bannock —
north-country bread of flour and water mixed with a pinch

of baking powder and fried in deer fat — made with dried blueberries. It was the best trail food either boy had eaten for many months and Jamie found himself thinking almost kindly of the black-haired, bright-eyed girl who waited at the cabin on Macnair Lake.

CHAPTER 4

Into Hiding

BEFORE THE MIDDLE OF MARCH Peetyuk was up and doing again. When Jamie and Awasin arrived back from one of their trips to the traplines, they found him entertaining Alphonse Meewasin and four other Crees. Alphonse and his companions were on their way south to the trading post and had stopped by to find out what the boys needed. Alphonse readily agreed to carry some of their furs south to the post to trade for a long list of supplies and equipment which the boys had already prepared for him. After a big supper of roast caribou cooked by Angeline (who moved about the cabin as unobtrusively as a shadow in the presence of her father and the other grown men), Alphonse stood up and began to examine the furs stored in the rafters.

"We will take no good furs to the post," he explained. "The price is low there — and it is the same for good and bad. I myself will send the best furs out to The Pas in early summer. We will return in two weeks' time bringing the things you need. And when we come we will take the girl back to our camp." He paused and glanced poker-faced at

Peetyuk, "You must be worn out with her chattering tongue and tired of her lazy ways."

Before he could stop himself, the impulsive Peetyuk burst out in Angeline's defense. "She *not* lazy girl! She never talk too much. She very kind and good . . ."

He stopped abruptly as he saw the broad smiles spreading over the faces of the five men. As for Angeline, she banged the kettle down on the stove so hard the top leaped off it, and then she ran swiftly out of the cabin, slamming the door behind her.

Jamie was grinning too. "Oh well, I suppose we can put up with her," he said. "I suppose we *have to*, to keep Pete in a good mood."

"I think you had better take my sister home," Awasin disagreed. "If you do not, Peetyuk will never find himself well enough to leave the cabin and go trapping. Yet, it is strange, he is very strong for cutting wood and filling water pails . . ."

Goaded beyond measure, Peetyuk, jumping to his feet, caught Jamie around the neck with one arm, and Awasin with the other. "Yes," he shouted in exasperation, "and I strong to hit your heads together too . . . like this!" With which he gave them such a knock that they yelled with pain, while the Cree men burst into roars of laughter.

Alphonse stepped to the door and called his daughter. When she came reluctantly into the circle of light he patted her on the shoulder, tilted her small chin with his big hand, and looked down at her. "You are your mother's daughter," he told her, "and she is a good woman. It was a good thing you did when you came to a sickness camp. We do not mock you. If you wish to stay, and if these young men are willing, then you may stay, for it is hard for men to do their own work and do a woman's work as well."

Next morning the Cree party left for the south carrying a heavy load of furs as well as a long letter from Jamie to his uncle. Life at the Macnair cabin began to settle down. Peetyuk was soon able to take over his old trapline and he and Jamie shared Awasin's line between them, leaving the Cree boy free to take over Angus Macnair's long trapline to the north.

The boys trapped harder than they had ever done before. They were seldom at the cabin for more than a day at a time — just long enough for a sound sleep and some good meals cooked by Angeline, and to skin and prepare their catches. Luck, which had turned its face against the northern people for so many weeks, now relented. The catches were uniformly good. There were many martens and cross-breed foxes, and to cap it all Peetyuk caught a silver fox.

The boys were seldom all at the cabin at one time, and there was not much opportunity to talk and plan, or even to think about the future. Occasionally Jamie wondered how the authorities were taking his refusal to go "outside," but he did not worry overmuch about the matter.

Then on a day late in March Jamie returned from his trapline to find Alphonse and his men at the cabin. Only Awasin was absent when they all sat down to a meal. While they ate, Alphonse told Jamie and Peetyuk about the trading.

"The post manager was surprised we had so much fur and could buy so many things. But I do not think he could guess that much of what we bought was for you, and for the long trip to the Barrens. But he and the missionary asked many question about you, Jamie. Before we went away the missionary told me that we Crees must not keep you, or we would have big trouble with the police. We do not care about that. But he said a thing I did not like. He said the police will make a dog-team patrol to look for you, and if they do not find you they will perhaps come in an airplane that lands on ice."

A spasm of fear gripped Jamie. "A dog patrol could come anytime and we'd have no warning till it was right here. Or a plane could land right in front of the cabin. They'd catch me for sure. What do you think we ought to do?"

The question was addressed to Alphonse, but Peetyuk answered it.

"Do? We go before they come. Time now begin trapping beaver, muskrat anyway. Why not we go north of Crees to muskeg country? Many beaver, muskrat there. Good hunting place for *tuktu* — for deer I mean. Winter nearly finished anyhow. We live in tents."

"That is said well, Peetyuk," was Alphonse's comment. "If you move to the north of us we can warn you if the police come. First they will look for you here. Then they will come to us. The Crees will tell them little, and that little will not help them much." He began to fill his home-made pipe. "But you do not need to live in tents. There is Kasmere's cabin on Kasmere Lake. He was a great chief, although of the Idthen Eldeli people. He built a great house on a high hill, with many windows so he could see all that moved for many miles across his country. When he died no one took that house for he alone of the Chipeweyans would live under a roof. I think Denikazi would let you use that house. I will go to his camp and ask. And when Awasin returns from his trapline, I think you must pack all that you need and journey north."

Alphonse left the next morning, and when Awasin arrived home the following day he found the cabin in a turmoil. Most of the supplies and gear the boys would need both for the spring hunting and for the northern trip were already tied up into bundles ready to be loaded on the carioles and sled. Alphonse, true to his word, had obtained permission for the boys to use Kasmere's cabin and he had sent two of his men to Macnair Lake, with their dog teams, to help with the move.

Fearing at any moment to see a police patrol appear on the ice to the south, Jamie was so impatient to get away that he was hardly able to explain to the bewildered Awasin what was happening. But it was not long before Awasin got things straight, and he pitched in to help with such good effect that the procession of dog teams was able to get away that very afternoon. By dusk they had reached the Cree cabins at Thanout Lake where they all spent the night. The following day they pushed on until they came to Kasmere House, which dominated the crest of a high point of land on the east shore of Kasmere Lake.

It was a remarkable house. It was built of upright logs

instead of horizontally laid logs, and consisted of three separate rooms. There were two windows in each wall and, since the house stood high on a cleared hill well above the level of the surrounding trees, the whole country for eight or ten miles about lay open to view.

The dogs had a hard time dragging the loaded carioles up to the hilltop and Awasin remarked that it was going to be quite a chore for whoever had to haul water from the lake. It was not until he spoke that the boys became consciously aware that Angeline, who had taken over the water job at Macnair Lake, was still with them.

In fact she had already got the cabin stove going and was busy sweeping out the accumulated debris of the years since Chief Kasmere's death.

With a look of bewilderment on his face Jamie turned to stare at the open cabin door.

"Who said *she* could come?" he asked weakly.

No one answered. Angeline had certainly not been invited. On the other hand, no one had told her she could *not* come, either. In the confusion and hurry of the departure, and of the journey, Awasin had taken his sister's presence for granted. Peetyuk had been fully aware of her, but he was not the one to draw attention to her, or to suggest that she be left behind at the Cree camp. As for Jamie, he had been far too preoccupied with the urgent need to get away from Macnair Lake to notice her unobtrusive presence.

Awasin grinned a little ruefully. "Well," he said, "she's here, and if you know a way to get rid of her you can try your luck. As for me, I would as soon she stayed. Someone must do the cooking and she does not poison us like you two do when you get at the stove." He turned slyly to Peetyuk. "What do *you* think, Peetyuk? Is it not a good idea to have someone around to do the work while we sit back and rest?"

"What I think? I think I got to bang some heads again if you not leave poor girl alone."

"Poor girl!" Jamie snorted. "She's got you two wound right round her finger. But I'm outvoted, so I suppose she can stay, for a while at least."

Angeline seemed unaware of the discussion taking place outside the cabin door. But as she continued with her sweeping she was smiling to herself.

The move proved to be a good one for several reasons. Not only did Kasmere House offer safety from a surprise visit by the police, but the hunting grounds in the vicinity were excellent. These grounds belonged to the Chipeweyans, but the weakened survivors of the epidemic were not able to do any trapping that spring.

Two or three days after the boys and Angeline had settled in at Kasmere House they had a visit from Chief Denikazi. At first the old man did not say much, but he made them free of the house and of the Chipeweyan lands. In return (and at Awasin's suggestion) the boys volunteered to give the Chipeweyans a quarter of their muskrat and beaver catch, since they knew all too well how destitute the Chipeweyans were. If Denikazi was grateful for the gesture, he did not say so directly.

"In the hatching-moon you go north to the plains?" he

asked. "You not take white men's canoes. No good. Too heavy. You take Idthen Eldeli canoes. That is my word."

"I think he means," said Awasin translating, "that he intends to give us some Chipeweyan birchbark canoes. If that is true we are in luck. They are the finest canoes in the north. Very small and very light."

"Listen, Awasin," Jamie said. "Can you warn him about the police coming to look for me? He'd better know about it in case they come his way."

Awasin translated this and the dour old man's face lighted up with something approaching a grin. A spate of words poured from him.

"It is said the white police, they are great travelers. Eeeee! But beside *my* people they are trees rooted to the ground. They travel only on the broad roads, the big rivers and lakes. *My* people travel by ways only the deer have seen. The Idthen Eldeli will show you the hidden ways and then the white men can search till they grow old and lose their teeth, they will find nothing but gulls and squirrels. Eeeee! I will make more false trails for them than an old wolf."

April came and brought with it the first warnings of the thaw which would begin in May. The sun grew steadily hotter and the days longer. The boys set their spring traplines in the marshes and bogs and soon Kasmere House was festooned with stretchers carrying muskrat and beaver pelts. Once again life settled into a comfortable routine. The spring trapping was not as hectic as that of winter since the lines were much shorter. There was time for talk and even for occasional visits to the Cree cabins at Thanout Lake. The Crees were keeping a sharp lookout for any sign of strangers in the country, but so far they had seen nothing and heard nothing.

As the time of the spring break-up grew nearer, the fear of a police patrol faded. The boys knew that from mid-May until mid-June the opening rivers and the rotting ice on the lakes would prevent either dogsled or canoe travel from the south. By the time the canoe routes were open, the boys intended to be well started on their journey and beyond any serious danger of pursuit.

However, Jamie had discovered something new to worry about. On several occasions Peetyuk had managed to beat the other boys back from the traplines, somewhat to the detriment of his catch of muskrat. Each time when Jamie and Awasin returned home, they found him happily engaged in domestic tasks that were really a woman's job. On one occasion he had an old flour sack tied around his waist and was drying dishes for Angeline. Another time they found him lugging two big baskets of wet laundry up from the lake shore where he had built a fire and boiled a tub so that Angeline could do the wash without having to carry water all the way up the hill.

When Awasin teased him about these things Peetyuk seemed to lose his usual good nature and to become grouchy, so that Awasin finally gave up tormenting him. But Jamie grew steadily more concerned. If, as he suspected, Peetyuk was becoming sentimental about Angeline it posed a possible threat to the plans for the summer journey to the Barrens, and Jamie was determined that

nothing should be allowed to interfere with that trip.

A few days after the washtub incident it was decided that they should make a run to Thanout Lake to visit the Crees and to collect some new moosehide moccasins. Jamie had secretly decided that when they returned to Kasmere Lake after the visit it would be without Angeline, but he reckoned without the girl's powers of intuition. She resolutely refused to accompany them, claiming that there was so much mending and cooking to do that she could not go. Nothing, not even Peetyuk's rather pathetic efforts, would make her change her mind. In the end the boys had to go without her, but Jamie was in a highly irritable mood.

They stopped to brew up a billy can of tea at the still

frozen Kasmere Rapids. The water was just beginning to boil when Jamie burst out:

"Listen, you two. It's already May. In a week or two we ought to be starting north. It's time we got rid of Angeline. She's been okay around the cabin and all that, but now she's a nuisance. She's starting to act like she's one of us. Next thing we know she'll want to go north with us too."

"She cannot go north with us, Jamie," said Awasin soothingly. "We all know that. What harm is there if she stays at Kasmere House until we leave? My father will take her back home then."

"I'll tell you what harm," Jamie shouted, losing his temper entirely. "That fathead over there" — and he pointed at Peetyuk who was bending over the tea billy — "has gone nuts about her. He's not pulling his weight on the traplines or anywhere else and he goes around like he was about half drunk and useless all the time. What's he going to be like when we go north, eh?"

The ferocity of the outburst stunned Awasin, but it cut Peetyuk like a knife thrust. He straightened up and turned toward Jamie.

"You my friend," he said slowly. "Now you change. Angeline my friend too. She not change like you. You make you my enemy, then I be yours. You want fight, I fight."

Instantly Jamie was on his feet. "Why, you 'husky' idiot!" he shouted. "You need some sense beat into you!"

Before Awasin could make a move to intervene, the two had flung themselves on each other. It was a no-holds-barred struggle. Locked together they rolled into and over the fire, spilling the tea and scattering the coals in all directions. Jamie had hold of Peetyuk's mop of hair and was trying to pound his head against the gravel, while Peetyuk had his legs locked around Jamie's waist and was squeezing for all he was worth.

Awasin jumped back and forth trying to get a grip on them and pull them apart, but they ignored his efforts, grunting and snarling like two wild animals.

Suddenly Awasin stepped back and stood with his head cocked toward the south, a look of perplexity on his face.

"Stop it now!" he shouted. "*Stop that!* Be quiet! Listen! *What is that noise?*"

The urgency in his voice reached the fighters. Their struggles ceased and they sat up. Peetyuk's face was streaming with blood from a cut on his cheek. For a moment no one moved, then Jamie yelled: "The dogs! Get the dogs and sleds! We've got to hide! Hurry up for heaven's sake! *That's the engine of a plane!*"

CHAPTER 5

Flight to the North

THE DOGS HAD NOT BEEN UNHITCHED and it was only the work of moments for the three frightened boys to leap to their teams and guide them into the thick fringe of black spruce which stood only a few yards back from the frozen river. The fire was already out, leaving no tell-tale smoke to mark the stopping place, but Awasin, nevertheless, rushed back from the woods to kick snow over the black spot where it had burned. He had barely regained the shelter of the woods when the low-pitched whine which had first caught his attention, and which had been rapidly swelling in volume, became a deep-throated roar.

Crouched beside their dogs, the boys peered fearfully up through the branches as a ski-equipped, single-engine Norseman plane thundered over them at an altitude of no more than three hundred feet. The plane seemed so close Jamie imagined he could feel the eyes of its occupants looking straight down at him, and involuntarily he hid his face and crouched still lower in the snow. As he did so he remembered, with a sickening sense of panic, that while the sleds themselves were hidden their tracks were not.

The roar of the plane faded rapidly away, but when Jamie spoke it was in a whisper.

"They'll see our tracks. They'll see them and come back! We're caught . . . we'll never get away . . ."

Peetyuk was sitting back on his haunches, absently rubbing the blood off his cheek. He did not seem to have heard Jamie at all. His eyes, wide with wonder, were fixed on the pallid blue sky fretted with the tops of ragged spruces, where the plane had disappeared. This was the first plane he had ever seen and for the moment he was speechless with amazement. But Awasin, though he too had never seen a plane before, was as alert and quick as ever.

"I do not think so, Jamie. How can they tell which way the tracks lead? And how can they tell they are ours? But in case they do come back we must not stay near the river where the plane can land."

The calm voice of his friend washed away Jamie's panic.

"Come on then, let's get moving quick."

Awasin got to his feet and began to untangle his dog's traces, which had become hopelessly snarled during the wild rush for cover.

"The plane must have come to Macnair Lake first," he said thoughtfully. "Then it would have gone to my people's camp. My people would have said nothing of where we were. This is a big country, Jamie, and unless someone has talked about us to them they can only search like blind ones. But we cannot go to Thanout Lake now. The plane will probably stop there again on its way back. I think we must return to Kasmere House. If the plane is waiting for

us there we will see it in good time, for it is clear weather
and there will be a moon."

Peetyuk roused himself from his trance of wonder.

"If they make trouble with Angeline, I kill them all!" he
said, and from the tone of his voice there was no doubt
that he meant it.

Jamie gave him a sharp look. "Stop worrying about *her*,
Peetyuk. They won't hurt her. Look, we've got big trouble.
I'm sorry about the fight. I never really meant what I
said . . . it's just that I was nervous about things. Let's
forget it. Okay, Pete?"

Peetyuk beamed. "I forget quick. Now we friends again.
Much better we be friends."

The tangle of spruce along the riverbank was not very
broad, and half an hour later the boys emerged from it
into fairly open country, studded with jackpines, where
they could make good progress over the deep but firmly
crusted snow. They swung north, paralleling the river and
the east shore of Kasmere Lake. By late afternoon they
were only two or three miles from Kasmere House.

Leaving Jamie and Peetyuk with the dogs, Awasin went
on alone to the shore of the lake, moving cautiously so that
the tracks of his snowshoes would never cross open
ground. In an hour he was back with his waiting friends.

"There is no airplane and I could see no tracks on the
lake to show it had landed. But there is no smoke from the
chimney either, and I saw no sign of Angeline."

Peetyuk was on his feet in an instant, but Jamie caught
his arm.

"Don't be crazy, Pete. Probably she saw the plane or heard it and put out the stove so the police wouldn't see the smoke. Now listen, you two. We'll take the dogs to the south side of the hill and tether them in the woods. That way they'll be ready if we have to get out in a hurry. Then we can sneak up to the cabin and see what's happened."

It took only a few minutes to circle around the hill and tether the dogs. The boys climbed cautiously toward the cabin. When they were only a few yards from it Awasin whistled softly, but there was no answer and no sign of life. Jamie advanced to the side wall and peered in through the window.

"Nobody here," he said in astonishment. "Nobody at all. Angeline's gone."

Abandoning all caution, they ran around to the door. It was barred and nailed shut. Deeply puzzled and not a little frightened, they pried off the bar and pushed inside.

The cabin was clean and tidy — but deserted. Furthermore, and despite a strong and acrid smell of woodsmoke, it looked as if it had been deserted for days or weeks. Completely bewildered, the three boys poked through the various rooms and discovered that all their travel gear and supplies had vanished. The cabin was now almost as bare and empty as when they had first arrived at it weeks earlier. All of them felt a prickling of their scalps as they stood in the silent, empty house.

"I don't understand," Jamie said in a low voice. "How could Angeline and all our stuff just vanish like this? There's no sign of a fuss. It's like the place just hasn't been lived in for a dog's age . . ."

Peetyuk started for the door, his rifle in his hand and his face dark with fear and anger. "I not know what happen, but I find out!" he cried.

Awasin stepped in front of him but Peetyuk shoved him to one side. At that instant there came a noise which paralyzed the three of them. It was the ghostly sound of muffled laughter.

Jamie spun on his heel as if he had been shot, and there, with her nose pressed tight against the glass of the back window, and staring in at the boys with mischievous eyes, was Angeline.

Her story, when she got a chance to tell it, was simple enough. She had been outside cutting wood when she heard the unfamiliar roar of the Norseman's engine. Moments later she had seen the red and silver plane appear above the distant mouth of the Kasmere River. Running inside she had flung open the stove, raked the burning logs out onto the floor and doused them with water, thereby filling the cabin with smoke and steam and nearly suffocating herself. Coughing and gasping, she had grabbed her snowshoes and slipped outside again, intending to run into the bush and circle until she could safely pick up the boys' trail on the river ice and follow them. But when she came out she saw that the plane had made a turn and was disappearing into the northwest in the direction of the Chipeweyan camp.

Immediately Angeline changed her plans. There was a small hand-sled outside the cabin. Working with the fury of desperation, she began packing the boys' and her own

belongings, throwing them on the sled, and hauling them
down the slope into the woods on the north side of the hill.
When she finished that task she swept and cleaned the
cabin, doing everything she could to make it appear that it
had not been lived in for a long time. Then she took a
birch broom and smoothed the snow around the cabin to
remove her own tracks. She descended to the woods and
began laboriously hauling the equipment and supplies
deeper into the bush to the north. She slaved at her task all
that long afternoon until she had moved the gear to a
cache nearly two miles distant. She covered this cache
with spruce boughs, then she returned to the hill and hid
herself where she could watch the front of the cabin. By
this time she was utterly exhausted, and without meaning
to she dozed off, wrapped in her caribou-skin robe.

She woke to the sound of the cabin door being pried
open. Not sure who the new arrivals were, she crept cautiously to the edge of the woods where she saw and recognized the dogs. Relieved as she was to know that the boys
were safe, she had not been able to resist the impulse to
sneak up and surprise them.

Awasin looked at her affectionately when she had finished her story. "Our father spoke the truth," he said. "You
are a good girl, and very smart."

Beaming with unconcealed admiration, Peetyuk grabbed
the girl by the arm and spun her around so they both faced
Jamie. "*Very* good friend, this!" he shouted. "Now we *all*
very good friends, yes, Jamie?"

Jamie could not help smiling. "Sure, Pete. And Awasin's
right; you're a smart girl, Angeline. If the plane comes

here now they'll never know where we've gone or even if we were ever here." The smile vanished suddenly. "Angeline, do you think they saw the smoke before they turned?"

"I cannot tell, Jamie. There was a big fire to heat the washing water, and the cabin stands high. But the smoke did not last long. It was soon all inside the house, and inside me."

"They *could* have seen it, though," Awasin said thoughtfully. "We had better get away from here, I think."

"No need to panic," Jamie replied. "Those kind of planes don't fly at night and it's already dusk. Let's get our robes and some grub off the sled. We'll have a feed and make some plans."

Glowing under the unaccustomed praise from Jamie, and feeling proud of her own competence and happy in the results of it, Angeline hurried to light a fire — a small one of clear, dry wood. Meanwhile, the boys brought in their things. It was a cold night and the warmth of the cabin was pleasant, but even after they had eaten, and even though the room was dark (for they had thought it unwise to show a light), none of them felt the least bit sleepy. They were too much on edge to rest, and there was too much to talk about. However, although they discussed their situation for a couple of hours, they were unable to agree on any definite plan of action. Two things seemed certain — they could not remain at Kasmere House after daylight came. Nor could they go to Thanout Lake, at least until they knew for certain that the plane had left the

country. Peetyuk was of the opinion that they should start
north for the Barrenlands at once.

"Why we wait? Have all we need. With our good dogs
we go quick. Get to Eskimo country before ice begin to
melt. Police not find us then even he got one hundred
planes."

Awasin was against the idea.

"It is no good," he said doggedly. "We have still some
things to get at Thanout Lake, and most important we
have no canoe. How can we travel on the Barrens in summer without a canoe? How can we get back south in the
autumn without one? If we have only dogsleds we must
stay in the Barrens until winter before we can travel south.
And there is Angeline. We cannot leave her alone here to
walk back to Thanout Lake. Also I do not wish to go without telling my father and my mother. Many times I have
worried them very much, and I will not do this again."

Jamie was torn between the two. Much as he wanted to
get started north, and greatly as he feared being found by
the police, he recognized the truth of what Awasin said.
The argument was still going on when Angeline stepped
quietly outside, returning almost instantly to announce:

"Awasin! There is someone coming on the lake!"

The boys leaped up and ran outside. There was a hazy
moon giving just enough light to show that something
very odd was moving soundlessly across the lake toward
the hill. The head of it looked like a team of dogs, but
behind was a huge, looming shape beside which they
could just distinguish the running figure of a man.

"What on earth is it?" Jamie asked in sharp alarm.

"Never mind what. We must get away from the cabin," Awasin replied urgently. "Is the fire out, Angeline? Good. Move quick, the rest of you. We'll hide below the hill!"

Five minutes later they had gained the shelter of the forest and were crouching beside their teams, muttering hoarse threats to the first dog that dared open its mouth. They waited tensely and soon they could hear the squeaking of sled runners, the panting of dogs, and the flap-flap-flap of snowshoes. Then silence fell.

For what seemed hours the silence was unbroken. Peetyuk was about to stand up to take a look when, with heart-stopping suddenness, a figure loomed right over them and a sibilant voice cut through the night air.

With a gasp of relief Awasin jumped to his feet.

"It's all right. It is one of the Chipeweyans. He's come to tell us something."

In some embarrassment the four emerged from their hiding place (to which the Chipeweyan had tracked them easily) and joined their visitor. He proved to be a young hunter named Zabadees, and the mystery of the strange appearance of his team out on the lake ice was soon resolved. He had brought two fourteen-foot birch-bark canoes tied one on top of the other on his long sled.

Back in the cabin once more Awasin lit a candle. "It is safe now," he reassured his friends. "This man says the plane is at the Idthen Eldeli camp for the night, and the white men are sleeping in a tent beside it."

"Find out the rest!" Jamie cried impatiently.

For several minutes Awasin and Zabadees talked rapidly together, then Awasin translated.

"There are three white men. One is a policeman. One flies the plane. One is a doctor. The plane also brought Madees — the Chipeweyan who went south for help and almost died at Reindeer Lake. The white men made him guide them north. He did not know there was any trouble. But when they got to Thanout Lake my father managed to talk to Madees and tell him what was happening. My father also sent a message by Madees to me. He said we are to cache our furs and go north now if we can. He said the policeman was angry that you were not at Macnair or Thanout Lake. He thinks they will now search hard for you. He said we are to send Angeline to Denikazi's camp, and he will come for her there in a few days' time.

"Denikazi also sent a message. He too says we are to go north quickly. He sent the two canoes for us, and Zabadees is to go with us to the edge of the Barrens and show us the secret ways. He says the white men saw the smoke from the cabin and in the morning they may come here looking. Se we must go at once."

Jamie and Peetyuk bombarded Awasin with questions and he translated them to Zabadees — but the Chipeweyan could not add much to what he had already said except to say that Denikazi had been as good as his word, and had arranged to lay a false trail. A second Chipeweyan team had quietly slipped away from the camp with Zabadees after the white men went into their tent. The two teams had traveled together by a roundabout route almost to Kasmere Hill, where the second team had turned off. It was even then being driven up the center of the northwest arm of the lake and it would return the same way before dawn, thus leaving a trail which would appear to originate from Kasmere House. In all likelihood the police plane would follow this false trail. Meanwhile Zabadees was to lead the boys across country over a system of little ponds to the Putahow River. They were then to follow the Putahow north, traveling only at night for the first two laps of the journey.

"Denikazi's sure got it all planned out," Jamie said admiringly. "Sounds like a heck of a good plan too. What do you fellows think?"

"It is very good," Awasin answered. "But there is still one problem. What about my sister? We cannot leave her. Nor can she go to the Chipeweyan camp alone."

"No, and I will *not* go there anyway!" Angeline interjected firmly. "Perhaps they are good people, but I do not know them, and I will not stay with them. I will go with you."

"You will *not!*" Jamie snapped angrily.

Peetyuk, who had so far said very little, intervened.

"I not know *why* she cannot go, Jamie. She good cook, can paddle canoe, can drive dogs, can do most we can do. We got two canoes. Two fellows go in each. I mean" — he blushed a little — "two fellows in one canoe, one fellow and one girl in other canoe."

"No! By Harry!" Jamie cried in fury. "No girls!"

"Calm down, Jamie," Awasin said. "I know what we can do. She can go with us the first part of the way until Zabadees turns back. Then he can take her straight to Thanout Lake. I think he will agree to do that. I will ask him."

When the question was put to him Zabadees took his first real look at the girl. His sharp black eyes lingered on her attractive face and slim body for longer than Peetyuk liked. Finally the Chipeweyan looked back at Awasin and nodded his head.

"I will take her home," he said.

Since there was no real alternative, Jamie reluctantly agreed. An hour later the whole party was grouped around the cache which Angeline had made with so much labor. She had already tied up the stuff they were to take with them in travel bundles and so in a very short time the sled and carioles were loaded. Then, led by Zabadees's toboggan with its bulky cargo of canoes, the four teams took the trail through the moonlit jackpine forests into the waiting north.

CHAPTER 6

Zabadees

It was past midnight before they moved off, and that left little time to put a safe distance from Kasmere House before dawn. Nevertheless they were forced to travel slowly. Despite the light of the hazed moon it was hard to pick a trail through the dark stands of jackpine. The snow was deep and only lightly crusted, and the heavily laden carioles and sled kept breaking through the crust so that the dogs were soon panting with exertion. None of the party was able to ride. Even Zabadees, whose sled was lightly loaded (the canoes weighed only forty pounds apiece) was forced to walk ahead of his team to break a trail for them.

About 2:00 A.M. they reached the first of a chain of little lakes which they were to follow, and the going got better. Angeline, who had exhausted herself the previous day, was now so weary she could barely put one snowshoe ahead of the other. She kept up with the rest of them as best she could, and made no complaint. But when they stopped for a brief rest at the end of the first lake, Zabadees gave her a quick glance and spoke briefly to Awasin.

"He says his load is light," Awasin told his sister. "The going is better now, and he says you can ride on his sled. It would be wise to do that, for you will soon be too tired to keep up on foot."

Too weary to argue, Angeline obediently slipped off her snowshoes and climbed on the back of Zabadees's sled where she curled up with a deerhide over her.

The teams moved slowly over a low, spruce-covered ridge to the next lakelet. But when they were again on firm, smooth ice, the boys saw that Zabadees was rapidly pulling away from them. They thought nothing of it, for it was easy enough to follow his sled trail; but by the time they had reached the third in the chain of little lakes, he and his team were completely out of sight. They did not see him again until the opalescent light of dawn faded the setting moon and turned the dark blue snow to somber gray. By then they had reached and crossed a deep inlet of Kasmere Lake (staying close to the shore in order to hide their trail) and had come to another bay, from the end of which there was a portage into the Putahow River system.

Zabadees was waiting at the portage. Angeline was still sleeping soundly on his sled.

"He wants to know," Awasin told Peetyuk and Jamie, "if we should go any farther."

"I think we can risk another hour on the trail," Jamie replied. "They'll have to heat up their engine before they take off, and probably they'll eat first. Let's push on a bit. We're still too close to Kasmere House for comfort."

Zabadees nodded when he was told the decision. He

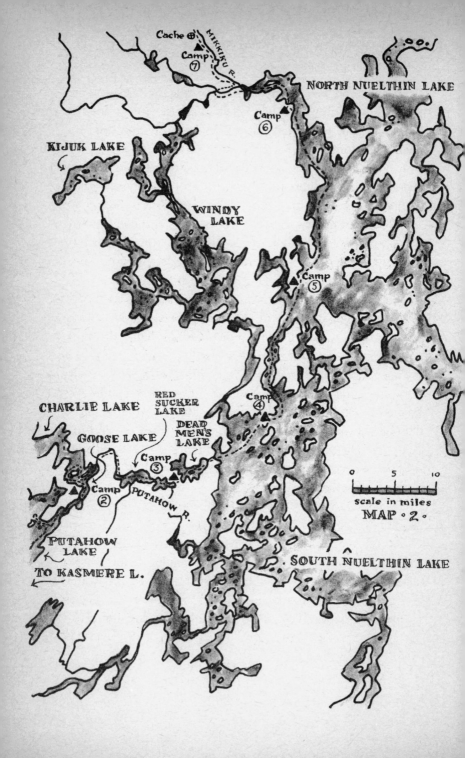

Cache ⊕

Camp
⑦

MIKKIKU R.

NORTH NUELTHIN LAKE

Camp
⑥

KIJUK LAKE

WINDY
LAKE

Camp
⑤

CHARLIE LAKE

RED
SUCKER
LAKE

DEAD
MEN'S
LAKE

Camp
④

GOOSE LAKE

Camp
③

Camp
②

PUTAHOW R.

0   5   10

scale in miles

MAP · 2 ·

PUTAHOW
LAKE

TO KASMERE L.

SOUTH NUELTHIN LAKE

called to his team and started off at once, leaving the boys to follow without having had time to rest either themselves or their dogs.

They caught up with him again on the fringe of a dense stand of black spruce beside the shore of the southern arm of Fisher Lake. He had already tramped down a trail into the heart of this thicket and soon the teams and sleds were well concealed.

The morning broke clear and bright — ideal weather for flying. Keeping their ears cocked for the sound of an aircraft engine, they had a cold breakfast of bannocks and boiled caribou meat. They were all bone-weary, and after feeding the dogs they spread their sleeping robes on piles of spruce boughs and lay down. Peetyuk and Zabadees went to sleep at once, and Awasin and Angeline soon followed them. But Jamie was too tense to sleep.

For a long time he lay, half dozing. The swish of melting snow slipping off the branches of a spruce tree brought him wide awake, his heart pounding heavily. He tried to force himself to go to sleep, but he had hardly begun to doze again when the faintest of sounds — no louder than the hum of a mosquito — jolted him awake once more.

This time there was no mistake. He reached over and shook Awasin. The two boys sat silent, every nerve drawn taut, straining toward the distant sound. Almost imperceptibly it grew louder, and Jamie concluded, with a sick certainty, that the airborne searchers must have spotted their trail. Then, mercifully, the far sound began to fade. Soon there was nothing to be heard in all the silent land except the guttural cry of a raven soaring high in the empty sky.

"They followed the false trail, Jamie," Awasin said with a sudden outrush of pent-up breath. "It is all right now. They will not come our way."

The tension slowly ebbed and at last Jamie drifted into the dark depths of exhausted sleep. He did not wake again until the day was almost done and then he became sleepily aware of someone touching his face. It was Angeline. In her hand she had a pint mug filled with meat soup, for Awasin had risked lighting a small fire. She was smiling uncertainly at him.

Pushing up on one elbow, he took the mug and thanked her perfunctorily. As she turned from him he wondered what she really thought of him, and he felt his conscience prick a little.

During the second night the fugitives made good progress. Their route followed the Putahow, and the lake and river ice, covered with a hard layer of wind-packed snow, made for fast going. At Zabadees's insistent invitation, Angeline again rode the last part of the way on the Chipeweyan's sled, and once more he drew away from the three boys, so that they were nearly an hour behind him in reaching their next camp on the shores of Goose Lake.

A fire was already burning when the boys arrived. Zabadees was not in sight, but Angeline came running out from shore to meet them and they were surprised by the warmth of her greeting. Awasin, who knew his sister better than any of them, was mystified. It was unlike her to be publicly so demonstrative. But after a quick meal had been eaten and the rest of the boys had gone to feed their dogs, she drew him aside and whispered rapidly into his ear. As he listened, Awasin's face darkened. When, an hour later, Zabadees appeared suddenly from the woods having returned from an unsuccessful hunt for deer, Awasin did not greet him nor did Angeline offer to build up the fire and get him hot food and drink. Zabadees looked speculatively at the two Crees for a long moment, but he said nothing. Having rebuilt the fire, he heated his own meal, then carried it off to where he had unrolled his sleeping robes, some distance away from the others.

"What's the matter with Zabadees?" Jamie asked as he was getting into his own sleeping robes.

"Nothing," Awasin answered shortly. "The Idthen Eldeli are strange people. They do not mix easily with others."

"They not so strange," Peetyuk said. "That fellow he stay with Angeline too much. What for he always go ahead when she on sled?"

"He has a lighter load, that's all, Peetyuk," Awasin replied. "Anyway, she is well rested now. She will not ride his sled tonight. Now go to sleep, for there is a long road ahead of us."

But they did not start off again that evening. The bad weather which they would have welcomed the previous day came upon them now that they did not want it. A bitter northeaster had begun to blow. By dusk occasional snow flurries had turned to a steady, driving blizzard which made night travel out of the question. The boys pitched the travel tent and, with a big fire burning at the door, they and Angeline made themselves snug inside. Zabadees did not join them even though Jamie invited him in with hospitable gestures. The Chipeweyan's distant, almost hostile attitude was worrying Jamie.

"We must have done something to annoy him," he told the others as they snuggled under their robes in the little tent. "I don't like it. If he gets sore he might push off and leave us on our own, and we don't know the road."

"Let him go," Peetyuk said loudly. "We not need. Soon come out of trees to my country. I find way then."

"But we aren't out of the forests yet, Pete. We still need him. I wish I knew what was eating him. You got any idea, Awasin?"

Awasin and Angeline exchanged a fleeting glance; but Awasin shook his head.

"It is nothing. He will be all right. Do not worry about him, Jamie."

By morning the storm had blown itself out, and after a big breakfast and a leisurely second mug of tea they decided to move on in daylight. It was the best sort of day for traveling. The storm had hardened the snow and a bright sun was thawing the surface just enough so that the carioles and sled glided effortlessly over it. It should have been a day for a record run.

But the day seemed to be full of unexpected halts and setbacks. Twice Zabadees appeared to lose the proper route and made long detours into dead-end bays. Once he halted unexpectedly, seized his rifle, and went off into the bush for an hour in pursuit of what the boys were sure was a nonexistent deer. To make matters worse he insisted on stopping to boil the tea billy every hour or two.

Peetyuk, who was undisguisedly delighted to find that Angeline had chosen to walk with him at the end of the train, was unperturbed by the slow progress; but Jamie grew increasingly upset. Awasin said nothing, and his face remained expressionless.

About 3:00 P.M. they left the Putahow system at the east end of Red Sucker Lake and crossed a low ridge to the shores of a new lake which Zabadees, when he was pressed for its name, reluctantly told them was called Dead Men's Lake. It stretched off to the eastward, and in its center was a small, barren rock island. As they descended toward the lake out of the spruce thickets, Zabadees called a halt to the day's journey by stopping his sled and unhitching his dogs. In vain Jamie expostulated with him, through a rather uncooperative Awasin. Nothing would persuade Zabadees to continue on. Finally, when Jamie had reluctantly resigned himself to losing the rest of the day, Zabadees pointed negligently to Angeline and, in his sibilant language, muttered a few quick words.

Awasin's face betrayed nothing of his inner feelings.

"He says he wants Angeline to travel with him. He says there are bad spirits in this country, but she is good luck and makes it easier for him to find the way."

"Well, let her then," said Jamie in exasperation. "She

might as well ride as walk. If he believes that stuff about spirits and luck, she might as well make herself useful."

Awasin's face hardened. "She is my sister, not a dog! She does not wish to ride the sled." Then his expression softened. "I am sorry, Jamie, but it is better if she does not ride with him."

"Why not, for heaven's sake? She'll have to ride all the way back to Thanout Lake with him anyway."

Awasin turned away and began to pull the remains of a haunch of caribou off his sled.

"We are getting short on dog feed," he said, changing the subject. "I have seen much deer sign today. I think it is as well if we camp here and make a hunt."

Peetyuk had listened closely to the conversation, but had said nothing. There was a strange look on his face. It was no longer amiable. Suddenly he turned to Angeline.

"That fellow speak bad you?" he asked abruptly. "I think he make trouble with you. *Eema* — yes?"

Angeline shook her head so violently that her long hair whirled gleaming in the fading sunlight. "There is nothing wrong, Peetyuk. Come, help me gather wood. Or, please, will you cut some ice for tea water?"

Puzzled and annoyed, Jamie watched the pair walk away. "Girls!" he muttered almost viciously. Then he shrugged his shoulders and began to unload his cariole.

Zabadees sat motionless on his sled. His black eyes followed Angeline with an intentness which might have explained many things to Jamie, if he had been acute enough to observe and understand. But Jamie was too wrapped up in the driving urge to put distance between himself and

Kasmere Lake to be alert to the interplay between the Chipeweyan and the Crees.

It was a calm night, touched with the first signs of the spring thaw, and so they did not bother with the travel tent but simply climbed into their sleeping robes. No one was particularly tired and they began talking about the country they were passing through. Peetyuk told a story about how the Eskimos had once tried to establish contact with a white trader who had a post on Thanout Lake.

He described how the most powerful and active of the Eskimos, a man named Kakumee, undertook to make a journey to this trading post even though the Eskimos were in mortal fear both of the Chipeweyans and of the shadowed forests in which the Indians lived. Kakumee started out in mid-winter with a sledload of white fox pelts drawn by twelve great Eskimo dogs. He made fast progress south, following the western shores of Nueltin Lake which the Chipeweyans called Nuelthin-tua — Lake of the Sleeping Islands.

Reaching a certain bay, Kakumee turned up a river leading into the forest country and on his first night amongst the trees he built his camp on a low, rocky islet in a lake, which gave him good observation in all directions. Alone in what had always been enemy country, he slept very lightly indeed, and when just after dawn one of his dogs growled, he was instantly awake.

In the pale early light he saw seven teams of dogs and seven carioles swinging across the ice toward him. Kakumee recognized the approaching strangers as Chipeweyans, but made no move either to flee or to take up a defensive position. Instead he quietly lit his fire, put a kettle on to boil, and waited with empty hands as the carioles swept up to his islet and stopped on the ice.

There were nine Chipeweyans in the party. At first they kept their distance, but when they had assured themselves that Kakumee was alone they came up to his fire. One of them insolently flung back the hides covering Kakumee's load of furs. Another kicked one of Kakumee's dogs, and when the animal lunged at him he struck it across the head with the butt of his rifle.

Kakumee could speak no Chipeweyan, but he could guess what the Indians were saying. When three of them casually began to rip open his bales of furs, while three others moved slowly around the fire so they would be behind the Eskimo, he wasted no more time.

He had concealed his .44-.40 repeating rifle under the loose folds of his parka. Without any hesitation, and so rapidly that the Chipeweyans could not have stopped him even if they had realized what he was up to, he flipped the rifle to his hip and shot the nearest Indian through the stomach. Even as this man screamed and fell, Kakumee whirled and shot one of the three who had tried to get behind him.

The remaining Chipeweyans panicked. They sprinted for their carioles while Kakumee methodically fired .44-.40 slugs into the ice right behind them. In ten minutes they had reached the far shore where they vanished into the forests, leaving the Eskimo in possession of his life, his furs, and two corpses. Abandoning the bodies where they had fallen, Kakumee continued on his way, reached the trading post, and returned safely home. Word of his exploit spread like fire through the forests and he saw no more Chipeweyans either then nor on later journeys south.

While Peetyuk was telling this story Zabadees seemed to pay no attention, but at several recurrences of the name "Kakumee" his gaze flickered toward Peetyuk. Peetyuk had observed this.

"That fellow he know story, I think. Awasin, you tell him what I tell. Also tell him all happen right on this lake, and tell him Kakumee my grandfather."

With evident relish Awasin translated the gist of the tale. He could see that it made Zabadees markedly uneasy. The Chipeweyan's gaze kept shifting from Awasin to Peetyuk, and when Awasin mentioned Peetyuk's relationship to Kakumee, Zabadees slipped out of his robes, spat angrily on the dying fire, and stalked off into the dark forests. He did not reappear until all except Peetyuk were asleep.

When the Chipeweyan eventually returned and slipped into his robes, Peetyuk got up and threw some sticks on the embers of the fire. When there was enough of a blaze to see by, he got his rifle from the cariole and methodically began to clean it. Every once in a while he cast a long, thoughtful look in the direction of the dark shadows which showed where Zabadees lay rolled up in his robes.

Then Peetyuk began to sing an Eskimo song, almost — but not quite — under his breath. It was a weird, alien chant that sounded as if it could easily have been an invocation to the dead. It rose and fell with nerve-wracking monotony. At intervals the name "Kakumee" occurred in it, and each time he chanted the name, Peetyuk clicked the bolt of his rifle.

In the dim and flickering light of the little fire his performance was immensely effective. By the time the fire died down and blackness returned, Peetyuk was chuckling to himself. "That is *one* Chipeweyan who will not sleep well tonight," he thought with satisfaction as he curled up comfortably under his robes.

CHAPTER 7

Nuelthin-tua

JAMIE SLEPT RESTLESSLY AND WAS
the first to waken. He lay quiet for a while, enjoying the
warmth of the robes, then he sat up and looked about him.
Awasin and Angeline were asleep with the carioles provid-
ing a windbreak for them. On the other side of the dead
fire Peetyuk lay completely buried under a mound of
robes. Zabadees was gone.

For a moment Jamie attached no significance to the
Chipeweyan's absence, thinking he had gone hunting or
was off gathering wood. Then he realized that Zabadees's
sleeping robes were missing. He scrambled out of his own
robes and stood up, looking toward the dog-lines down by
the lake shore. Zabadees's dogs were gone . . . and so
was his sled. The two canoes lay where they had been
hastily dropped on top of a snowdrift.

"Wake up!" Jamie shouted urgently. "Wake up, you fellows! Zabadees has done a bunk!"

Peetyuk's head popped out from under his robes, his red
hair awry. "Where bunk?" he asked, puzzled. "Here no
cabin. Here no bunk."

"He's *gone*, you idiot!" cried the exasperated Jamie. "Awasin! Wake up!"

The three boys hurriedly pulled on their stockings and moccasins and ran together to the shore of the frozen lake. There was no doubt about it. They could plainly distinguish the tracks of Zabadees's sled overlying those they had made the previous day.

"Come on," Jamie cried urgently. "Let's get a team hitched up. Maybe we can catch him."

Awasin, who had been examining the trail, replied quietly. "I think not, Jamie. He has been gone many hours. And if we did catch him, how could we turn him back?"

Jamie was beside himself. He turned fiercely on Peetyuk.

"This is *your* fault!" he shouted angrily. "You and your fool yarns. You must have scared the wits out of him with that story and he took off. *Now* how are we going to find the road . . . and," a blank look spread across his face, "how do we get rid of Angeline?"

Peetyuk replied rather meekly. "I sorry, Jamie. Not know he so big coward. Only I wish make him leave Angeline alone. He bother her too much."

"That is true," Awasin cut in. "And there is more than Peetyuk knows. I would not tell either of you before. *You* would have been angry at Angeline, and Peetyuk might have made real trouble with Zabadees. Two days ago when he went so fast ahead of us, he said things to Angeline. I do not blame him too much. He is a young man, and the girl he would have married died of the lung sickness this spring. So he wished to take Angeline and make her his wife. When he found she would not have him, maybe he did not want to help us anymore. Anyway, it is a good thing he is gone. If you had said she had to go back with him I would have taken her home myself."

"I wish I shoot hole in his head!" Peetyuk blazed. Then a slow smile spread over his face. "I guess he *think* I shoot — like Kakumee. Listen, I tell what happen . . ." and he described the charade he had acted out for Zabadees's benefit.

Awasin chuckled and, despite himself, Jamie could not suppress a half-smile. Then his face clouded.

"That's fine and dandy fun for you, but we're in a real jam now. Not only are we stuck with Angeline, we don't have a clue about the route from here to the edge of the Barrens."

"Clue? What that?" Peetyuk asked. "Never mind clue. That story I tell, all true. I hear many times. Kakumee come this way. So we go east on Dead Men's Lake. It run into big lake Idthen people call Nuelthin, then go north. I find way easy."

Angeline had joined them as they talked and now she spoke directly to Jamie.

"I too am sorry, Jamie. I wished not to make any trouble, and I would never have told any but my brother what Zabadees was like. If you want me to go back, I will go alone on my snowshoes. I can carry enough food in a packsack."

Jamie bit back the sharp reply he was about to make, for he saw that the suggestion of tears glinted in the girl's dark eyes. "Listen, Angeline," he said awkwardly. "I don't think it's a good idea to take you into the Barrens. It can be awfully tough out there. But you sure can't walk back to Thanout Lake alone, so I guess you'll have to come with us."

Awasin and Peetyuk were both smiling as Jamie finished, Awasin from relief that a difficult situation had been eased and Peetyuk from pure delight. When, an hour later, they sat around the fire eating their breakfast of porridge, bannock and tea, they were a gay and purposeful crew — more cheerful than they had been for many days.

When they broke camp they did so with renewed enthusiasm. They rearranged the loads, placing some of the lighter gear from Peetyuk's long sled on the carioles, and tied the two canoes (nested one inside the other, with their thwarts removed) upside down on top of Peetyuk's sled. Angeline would drive Peetyuk's team in the lead position, while Peetyuk went ahead on snowshoes to find and break the trail.

The dogs seemed filled with new energy, too. The sleds moved off at a good pace and were soon abreast of the rocky islet. On its crest stood two gray clusters of poles, cone-shaped and looking somewhat like the skeletons of tepees. Awasin called to his team and the dogs broke into a run and drew up alongside Jamie's cariole.

"Old-fashioned Chipeweyan graves," Awasin shouted, pointing to the two "tepees." "Peetyuk's story must have been true."

Dead Men's Lake was not a long one and in an hour they had found its exit. There followed half an hour's swift

run down the ice of a small river, then suddenly ahead of
them lay an immense expanse of open ice stretching to the
eastern horizon.

The carioles and the sled came to a halt and the four
travelers stood together looking out over the vast reaches
of Nuelthin-tua. To the south the gray waste of ice lost
itself amongst innumerable wooded islands. To the north
there seemed to be just as many islands, but these were
barren of all trees. Black and rounded, they humped up
from the ice like the backs of so many sleeping mastodons.

"That where *my* land begin," said Peetyuk proudly,
pointing to the north.

"Then let's get moving," Jamie replied. "Look at that
sky. If we get caught in a blizzard out on the open ice we'll
have a rough time."

The almost colorless sky was streaked with long stream-
ers of white clouds which seemed to be fleeing, like a
school of silver herring, in front of an ominous dark mass
which was swelling up over the eastern horizon.

"Big storm, maybe," Awasin said. "It is better if we do
not go far from shore."

No one disputed the wisdom of this, and when they
started on again it was along the shore of what was evi-
dently a great bay which ran northward until it termi-
nated in a line of barren hills.

Soon the wind began to rise, kicking flurries of snow
crystals ahead of them. The sky darkened rapidly. By noon
it was completely overcast. Anxious to make as much distance as possible before the storm broke, they did not stop
for lunch but pushed on, munching pieces of cold bannock

as they trotted beside their sleds. Reaching the foot of the bay they turned east to skirt its hills and this brought the wind dead in their teeth. Suddenly the black clouds overhead began to disgorge not snow, as they had expected, but a bitter, driving rain.

They raced toward the nearby shore, but there was little shelter there. Gone were the thick spruce and jackpine forests of the Putahow country, leaving a scattering of small and wind-distorted trees. The only protection they could find was behind a cluster of frost-shattered boulders. By the time they had the tent up everything was soaking wet.

It was almost dark before the boys could gather enough twigs and brush for a fire, and when they eventually got it lit the wind and rain put it out again before they could even boil the tea billy. They gave up and crawled into the tent where Angeline had been doing what she could to arrange the drier robes for them to sleep under.

They spent a miserable night, but cold and uncomfortable as they were they were not unhappy. As the tent flapped and snapped under the assault of wind and rain, they sat huddled together with robes pulled over their shoulders and sang to keep up their spirits. Angeline had a particularly sweet, clear voice, and at her brother's urging she sang some songs she had learned at the mission school.

Only Peetyuk, that usually amiable and jovial youth, seemed subdued. When Jamie teased him a little, calling him a "gloomy-gus," he mustered a smile.

"Forest country — that your country," he explained. "*You* know that country and so *I* not worry there. Now we come *my* country. You not know so much. Now I worry for all. Soon rivers melting. After that ice go bad on small lakes. After that go bad on big lakes. If we not get to In-nuit camps soon, we stuck. This rain no good. Much water come in rivers."

"That's true," Jamie agreed. "But I guess we'll be all right on Nuelthin. It won't thaw for a long time yet. How far do we go on it, Peetyuk?"

"Maybe two-three days. After that must go on little rivers and lakes and over country."

"The rain is not so strong now," Awasin said. "Perhaps it will stop soon. We should try and sleep a little."

"Only a fish could sleep in this tent," Jamie grumbled. Nevertheless, it was not long before they were all dozing.

The morning broke dry and warm with a south wind blowing and clear skies overhead. Cold, stiff and tired, the four crawled out at dawn. Peetyuk got a fire going, and after a hasty mug of tea and some fried deermeat the travelers hitched up the willing dogs and moved off.

The rain had made shallow melt pools on top of the ice and had turned the overlying snow into thin slush. Nevertheless, it was good going for the sled and carioles, and the dogs seemed to share the impatience of their masters to get north. All that day they drove steadily on, stopping only twice to brew tea on willow fires at the shore and to have a bite to eat. Before noon they passed through a narrows into the northern part of Nuelthin-tua, and here they said good-by to the last trees. Ahead of them stretched the gigantic sweep of the Barrenlands, where the only wood they would find would be tiny clumps of willows huddled in the bottom of a few protected valleys.

When they pitched camp that night they had covered twenty miles, which, considering that none of them had been able to ride on the overloaded sleds, was a good day's run. And "run" was the right word, for the boys and Angeline literally ran much of the way.

The following day — their sixth since leaving Kasmere House — they made equally good progress. There was frost at night, but in the daytime the temperature rose well above freezing and the thaw continued. Peetyuk grew more and more concerned and he led them on at the fastest pace dogs and people could maintain. Their camp at the end of the sixth day was on the shore of a deep bay which ran off to the northwest from the main body of Nuelthin.

The hard pace had begun to tell on them and they took time only to gulp down a hasty meal before crawling into their robes. The dogs went hungry, for the supplies of caribou meat were almost exhausted and the boys had seen no deer all the way up the lake.

The spring-like weather seemed determined to persist. There was only a light frost that night and the morning sun rose white and hot in a cloudless sky. Once more Peetyuk got them moving almost before everyone was fully awake. "Sun too hot," he told them with a worried frown. "Maybe little rivers break ice already."

As they drove up the bay (which now swung almost due west) sled and carioles threw up a steady spray, for the thaw water on top of the ice was several inches deep in places.

"Good thing we have the canoes," Jamie remarked to Awasin, who was driving alongside. "Another day like this and we'll be using them. Either that or we'll have to teach the dogs to swim."

Awasin was about to offer a joke in reply when he saw that Peetyuk had turned and was running back toward them, holding up his hand to warn Angeline to stop. In a moment the other teams had drawn up to Peetyuk's sled.

"Get guns quick," he said urgently. "Around point, *tuktu-mie* — many deer. Angeline, you stay. Keep dogs quiet."

Slipping their rifles out of their deerskin cases, the boys ran swiftly for the cover of a long, low point of rock. When they reached the point they crawled slowly up to the crest and peered over it.

Ten feet below them, and not fifty yards away, the black ice of the bay almost disappeared under a flowing tide of caribou. Perhaps a thousand animals were in sight, strung out in long, twisting skeins, crossing the bay from south to north. They moved slowly and the boys saw that they were all does — most of them with swollen bellies, for the fawning time was almost on them.

Jamie and Awasin were so fascinated by the spectacle

that they did not even think of raising their guns. As a dozen skeins of deer crossed in front of them, others descended to the bay ice from the southern hills. Away to the north they could see that the rising hills in that direction were lined and veined with countless lines of caribou. Each skein — and some consisted of as many as a hundred animals — seemed to be led by an old doe, perhaps one who had made the thousand-mile spring migration a score of times before.

"Not wait all day," Peetyuk said impatiently. "We also must go fast north. I shoot now."

He eased his rifle up to his shoulder, took quick aim and fired. The flat crash of the shot echoed over the ice, but the mass of the deer seemed to pay little heed to it. One barren doe sank to her knees, struggled to rise again, and then fell over on her side. The rest of the animals in the file behind swerved slightly and passed by her. Here and there a few does halted for a moment, thrust their heads out in the direction of the point, snorted, and continued on their way.

"When does go north to fawn nothing stop them," Peetyuk explained. "Not afraid wolf, people. Not stop for anything."

He proved the point a few minutes later. Having returned to their teams, the boys and Angeline drove right into the deer herds. The hungry dogs nearly went mad. Jamie was caught off guard and lost control of his team, which went belting across the ice at full gallop, leaving him running far astern and bellowing uselessly at them to stop.

But the deer simply spread out to let the dogs go past, and when the team turned in pursuit of a single animal, the caribou only sprinted far enough to out-distance their pursuers before turning purposefully north at a sedate trot. Jamie's dogs now tried to run in all directions at once and their frantic efforts soon resulted in such a tangle of traces that they and the cariole were brought to a standstill. When Jamie panted up to them he found the lines so fouled that it took him twenty minutes of yelling, thumping and sweating to get the dogs disentangled. Meantime Awasin and Peetyuk had butchered and quartered the barren doe, flung the meat on their sleds, and driven on to join him.

Peetyuk shook his head sadly as he looked down at the tangled harness. "Maybe you be good driver some day," he said. "*Some* white men learn, but take long time. Got white beard by then."

Too winded to reply, Jamie could do nothing but grunt disgustedly as Peetyuk's sled swept past, heading toward the foot of the long bay.

CHAPTER 8

Race Against Time

THE NORTHWEST BAY OF NUELTHIN
ended in a snow-choked valley which wound away to the
westward between high, barren hills. Without slackening
pace, Peetyuk led the teams onto the ice of a river flowing
out of this valley. The surface was rough and pitted and in
places it had sagged, allowing thaw pools a foot in depth
to form on top of it.

They had gone several miles when Peetyuk halted the
train and went carefully forward, testing the ice with the
butt of his rifle. He came back in a few minutes looking
very worried.

"Rapid run under ice," he told the others. "Melt ice from
under. Too thin here. Must go shore."

"We'll never get anywhere along the shore," Jamie
protested. "The drifts in this valley must be ten feet deep,
and the snow's so soft a butterfly would sink in it."

"Maybe wrong river anyway," Peetyuk replied hesitantly. "This one go west, and big. River we want go
northwest, and not very big. Should go out over country,
not up big valley. Maybe I too much hurry. Maybe we go
back and look again."

It was a depressing prospect, but there was really no

alternative. They turned the sled and carioles about, and two hours later they reached the river mouth and were again on the bay ice. Here they halted while Peetyuk climbed a hill and scanned the north shore of the bay. When he scrambled down to join the others, his worried frown had been replaced by his usual grin.

"I find!" he told them jubilantly, and led them off toward a little cove concealed behind a string of islands. They did not see the river they were seeking until they turned a final bend.

"How did you ever find it, Pete?" Jamie asked.

"Not see river, Jamie. See *that* . . ." and he pointed to the crest of one of the masking islands. On the skyline stood a pile of stones set one on top of the other and no more than three feet high. To a casual eye the pile looked like a natural object, for the whole of the Barrenland plains are sprinkled thickly and haphazardly with jumbled rocks deposited by the retreating glaciers of the ancient past.

"He is *inukok* — stoneman," Peetyuk explained. "Eskimo make him. Make many *inukok* all over country. Show way to go for other Eskimo. I think Kakumee make that one. Got right road now."

Although the afternoon was growing old, Peetyuk would not let them stop even long enough to boil the kettle. Wearily the dogs took up the strain, and just as wearily the three boys and the girl plodded on.

This new river was not much more than a shallow stream winding its way up from the bay in a northwesterly direction over open, rolling plains criss-crossed with long gravel ridges completely free of snow. Innumerable small ponds and lakes lay in the snow-filled valleys, and the edges of these lakes had already thawed, leaving a narrow ring of open water between their shores and the rotting ice.

Mikkiku, or Little River, which was what Peetyuk called it, offered hard traveling. Not only was its ice rotten, but it was studded with boulders. There was a great deal of melt water on the surface, and the travelers could plainly hear the ominous mutter of a river in spate under the decaying ice.

The toboggan-like carioles were not well suited to these conditions, since they lay flat on the surface and tended to build up masses of heavy slush ahead of them. Everything aboard the carioles soon became soaked. On the other hand, Peetyuk's Eskimo-style sled, with its high runners, rode easily through the slush so that his load remained dry.

All four were soon soaked to the knees, and the bitter cold of the ice water chilled and numbed their legs. There were still two or three hours of daylight remaining when Angeline, who had gamely kept up with the rest and never uttered a word of complaint, slipped through a melt hole and plunged into the water to her waist.

Awasin quickly hauled her out and then declared that the day's journey was at an end.

"That is enough," he said wearily. "I know we must go fast, but we will kill the dogs if we go too hard."

Peetyuk gave in. "Okay, we camp. Good sand ridge here. Maybe find wood for fire."

Leaving the others to unload the carioles and spread the things to dry on the slope of a little sandy hill, he went scurrying off upstream and shortly returned carrying a huge armful of bone-dry, silver-colored sticks. "One time forest grow far out on country," he explained when they asked him where he had found this surprising windfall. "Long, long time ago trees die, I not know why. Wood stand up and never rot. Very good for fire."

These relics of a warmer climate and of the retreating tree line burned with a hot, white flame that sent steam curling from the moccasins, sleeping robes and stockings which hung over rocks and sticks all around the fire.

They ate a big meal of deer steaks fried in marrow fat and, since the sky was still clear, they decided against setting up the tent. Restored by good food, dry clothes and a rest, Jamie, Awasin and Angeline climbed to the top of the sand hill for a look at the surrounding country.

It was Angeline's first real look at the true Barrenlands and for a time she was silent in the face of the immensity of space, the vast panorama of rolling hills, rock ridges, and broad valleys that seemed to reach to the end of the world.

"I think I do not like it," she said softly, and shivered a little. "It is too big . . . and empty."

"It is not empty, sister," Awasin told her. "Do you see the many little dots that look like rocks? Watch . . . they move a little, eh? They are caribou. This is indeed the land of the deer. They come to us in the forests for a little while, in winter, but this is their land. When Jamie and I came north last year with Denikazi, we met so many deer sometimes we could hardly move among them. No, it is not an empty land."

Peetyuk, who had been feeding the dogs, joined them. He seemed to have undergone a physical change in the past day or two, and he looked bigger, more powerful, and more sure of himself. He stood beside them, his red hair stirring in the breeze and his head thrust forward toward the north like a questing wolf. The jovial, rather devil-may-care boy Jamie and Awasin had known during the winter had been replaced by a youth whose competence shone in his blue eyes and in the very set of his face.

"My country!" Peetyuk said proudly. "This is country of *tuktu*, and of Innuit. Deer and men. Is very good."

Jamie grinned and lightly punched his friend in the ribs. "Pete, you talk like a tourist guide. I tell you one thing. I don't think so much of the *roads* in your precious country."

Peetyuk did not return the smile. "Roads bad," he agreed. "We come too late. Carioles no good here. Too early for canoe. My people not move around this time of year. But *we* must move . . . move quick. Maybe better cache some stuff here."

"That is a good plan," Awasin agreed. "The ice melts swiftly now. We will not make ten miles a day with our full loads."

Returning to camp, they pitched into the job of spreading out the motley collection of gear and supplies and

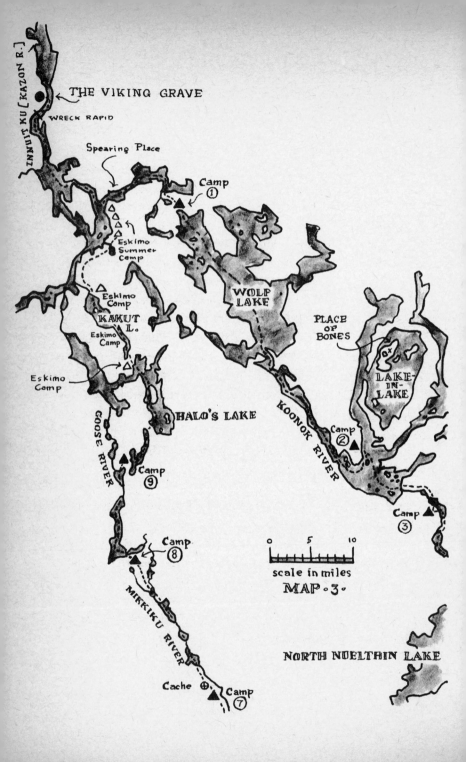

THE VIKING GRAVE

WRECK RAPID

INNUIT KU [KAZON R.]

Spearing Place

Camp ①

Eskimo Summer Camp

Eskimo Comp

KAKUT L.

Eskimo Comp

Eskimo Comp

WOLF LAKE

PLACE OF BONES

LAKE-IN-LAKE

KOONOK RIVER

Camp ②

Camp ③

HALO'S LAKE

GOOSE RIVER

Camp ⑨

Camp ⑧

MIKKIKU RIVER

Cache

Camp ⑦

0   5   10
scale in miles
MAP · 3 ·

NORTH NUELTHIN LAKE

sorting it into two piles — one to take and one to leave. The boys had brought two cases of rifle ammunition, several sacks of flour and three cases of tea as gifts for the Eskimos who had been so kind to Jamie and Awasin the previous winter when they had been lost in the Barrens. Most of these supplies, together with some tea, lard, flour, ammunition, spare clothes, and other things belonging to the boys, were placed high on the sand hill and securely covered with caribou skins weighted with rocks. Peetyuk explained that once the river was ice-free a party of Eskimos would be able to make a trip to the cache and ferry the contents back to the Eskimo camps in their kayaks.

The weather turned very cold that night, bringing a hard frost. The lightened carioles and sled made fast progress up the narrow, meandering channel of Little River. Before dark the party had reached the river's source and were on the height of land beyond which the rivers flowed northward. They camped in the lee of a high ridge upon whose crest stood several friendly-looking *inukok*.

"If stay cold, we come Innuit camps one day now," Peetyuk announced jubilantly.

But in the Barrens the weather is always unpredictable. That night the wind veered to southwest and became warm. Before dawn a heavy rain began to fall. When they began descending Tingmeaku, Goose River, the runoff from the saturated snows in the nearby valleys was so heavy that the river was flowing on *top* of the ice, as well as under it. In a short time everyone and everything was soaked. An attempt to leave the river and go across country was frustrated by the masses of soggy snow which filled the valleys. Reluctantly the travelers returned to the flooded river, but they could move on it only with the greatest caution, since the ice had become so thin it could barely support either sleds or people. Nevertheless, Peetyuk would not hear of a halt.

"Must go on," he told the others. "Any time ice begin break. Then finish travel with sleds."

Every few miles they had a brief respite when the river widened into a little lake, but even these small lakes were becoming dangerous to cross and several times the lead dogs broke through weak spots, necessitating long and careful detours.

By dusk they had not yet done with wading down Goose River, and again they had a cold and unpleasant camp. In the morning they were all so thoroughly miserable that Peetyuk had a hard time getting them to move at all. Sluggish, and dull with fatigue and chill, they finally started off. About noon the sky began to break, and shortly afterwards they saw ahead of them the broad expanse of a big lake.

"Halo Kumanik — Halo's Lake!" cried Peetyuk. "Now got no more trouble. Come on quick!"

With lightened spirits the travelers drove out onto this lake, having first had to bridge a narrow band of open water at the shore by means of Peetyuk's long sled. Floating free from the shore, the lake ice was dry and made ideal going. Even the dogs picked up heart. The train drove quickly northward. Late in the afternoon they passed through a narrows into another arm of the lake.

Peetyuk, who was well in the lead, gave a sudden shout. Catching the excitement in his voice, the others peered ahead.

"Look!" Angeline cried. "Up on that point! People and tents!"

On a long, low-lying point on the west shore stood five squat, conical tents. Although they were at least a mile away, the travelers could see signs of great activity about them. Dogs were chasing about in all directions and people were emerging from the tents and running toward the shore.

"You are right, Angeline," Awasin shouted breathlessly, for his dogs had caught the scent of the camp and had broken into a gallop. "Now, little sister, we meet Ayuskee-mos — the raw meat eaters. Make yourself brave in case they want to eat *you* up."

CHAPTER 9

The Ihalmiut Camps

Peetyuk's sled was the first to reach shore and it was immediately surrounded by such a throng of men, women, children and dogs that both it and Peetyuk seemed to disappear under a heaving brown mass. Having regained control of their own excited dogs Jamie and Awasin halted their teams a hundred yards away from the camp. Standing with Angeline between them, they observed Peetyuk's noisy reception, but made no move to join him.

Something more than shyness held them back. It was not exactly fear, for they knew they had nothing to fear from the Eskimos. Rather it was as if they had come out of one period in time and into another; rolled back innumerable centuries to enter a world and to encounter a people of unimaginable antiquity.

They had known before they started north that the inland Eskimos were an extremely isolated people who had never had more than peripheral contact with the world of white men. According to Peetyuk, only a handful of strangers had ever visited the Ihalmiut (People of the Little

Hills), as they called themselves. It was true that a few of the most intrepid Eskimos occasionally undertook the long journey to a trading post and, as a consequence, they had a few rifles and other trade goods. But for the most part the Ihalmiut lived as they had always lived, much as their ancestors had lived in times when Europe itself was a forested wilderness inhabited only by wandering hunters.

The sensation of having stumbled into an ancient and alien world was so strong that Angeline and the two boys had no idea how they should act, or what they should do. They might have stood out on the ice like statues for hours if Peetyuk had not pulled himself free of the yelling, laughing crowd and turned toward them.

"Why you stop?" he shouted. "You afraid Innuit? Foolish! Come quick and meet my people!"

Considerably embarrassed, Awasin and Jamie took hold of the traces of their lead dogs and led them toward the shore. Angeline followed so closely on Awasin's heels that she almost tripped him. To make the moment of meeting even more difficult, the assembled Eskimos became dead quiet, standing in a straggling row watching intently as the strangers slowly approached them.

Peetyuk ran forward calling to two Eskimo lads to join him. Putting one of the youths in charge of each team (so that a fight with the free-roaming Eskimo dogs would not develop) he grabbed Angeline by one hand and Jamie by the other and almost dragged them up to where the Eskimos stood waiting.

He took them straight to a bear-shaped, long-haired old

man whose broad, deeply seamed face was split by an immense smile showing the well-worn stubs of his brown teeth.

"This Kakut," Peetyuk said. "Like father with me after my father die."

Jamie grinned self-consciously and thrust out his hand, a gesture which clearly puzzled the old Eskimo. Obviously, he did not know what to do about that outstretched hand, and Jamie let it fall to his side. He blushed.

"I remember him from last winter," he said almost brusquely. "How do you do, Mr. Kakut?"

Peetyuk howled with mirth, bending almost double as he tried to control himself. When he straightened up he cried:

"Kakut he not big white man! He Eskimo! Not shake hands, not say 'How do.' Rub nose together! Like this."

Whirling Angeline around he thrust out his face and rubbed his nose back and forth against hers, whereupon a roar of laughter erupted from the watching people. The tenseness vanished and all the Eskimos pushed forward, milling around the strangers. Men and women touched them on the hands, patted their shoulders, laughed and gabbled until the noise was deafening.

"My gosh," Jamie muttered to Awasin. "How excited can you get?"

"They are going to scare Angeline to death, I think," Awasin replied. "Look, she has hold of Peetyuk like a drowning woman!"

The travelers were borne away toward the largest of the tents. It was made of scraped caribou skins sewed together in patchwork fashion and hung on a frame of light poles. Cone-shaped, it was about twenty feet in diameter at the base and stood about twelve feet high. The boys and Angeline were half escorted and half pushed through the door opening to find themselves in a roomy interior well lighted by the yellow glow of sunlight coming through the caribou hides. Caribou robes, fur side up, formed a thick mattress across the back half of the enclosed space. Pieces of skin clothing, caribou antler tools, a bow and arrow, and many unidentifiable objects hung from the supporting poles or littered the floor.

"Sit down," Peetyuk invited his friends. "Now big feed come. Always big feed for visitors, then much talk."

"Where is your mother, Peetyuk?" Awasin asked.

"She at camp on Kakut Lake," he replied, and went on to explain that the People were living in three separate camps at strategic points between Halo Lake and the Kazon River, which the Eskimos called Innuit Ku — the River of Men. The reason for this dispersal was so they would be stretched across the path of the northbound deer herds, and would thus have better opportunities to make a good kill.

"Have no bullets for guns," Peetyuk explained. "Must hunt with spear and bow. Not easy kill enough. People much hungry this winter."

He was interrupted by the appearance of a round-faced, smiling woman of middle age whose black hair was drawn back from her broad forehead and held in place by a gleaming copper ornament. She carried a deep wooden tray filled with soup, in which brown objects bobbed about. She set the tray in front of them and withdrew. The doorway was instantly filled by the heads of at least a dozen children, solemn-faced, round-eyed, and fascinated.

"Boiled deer tongues," Peetyuk explained. "We must eat all. This best food in camp. Give all to us. Eskimos sad if we not eat."

The tongues were delicious and the party was hungry, so there was no problem about obeying Peetyuk's instructions. But before the tray was empty two other women appeared. One carried an old pail and the other a tray. The pail was full of fishheads whose hard-boiled eyes gazed up smokily from the water they floated in. On the second tray was a heaping mound of roasted deer ribs.

"Ye gods!" Jamie exclaimed. "Do they expect us to eat all *that?*"

"Must eat," Peetyuk replied, "Eskimos give all food they have. Not want make Eskimos sad, Jamie."

"It'll make *me* sad, or dead. There's enough here for an army. And I wish those fish would shut their eyes. I hate being stared at when I eat."

Half an hour later, stuffed to the bursting point, Awasin, Jamie and Angeline gave up and leaned back on the caribou robes, gasping for breath. But not Peetyuk. Clean-gnawed caribou ribs continued to fly from his right hand to the door, where the watching children ducked to let them pass and the dogs pounced on the bones and carried them away.

The people of the camp now began to drift into the tent in ones and twos. Soon Peetyuk was too busy talking to continue with his feast. He had much to tell the Eskimos, and they had much to tell him, for it had been nearly six months since he had left them to journey south with Jamie and Awasin to the forest lands.

Jamie, Awasin and Angeline were left out of it for the moment — which suited them very well. The respite gave them time to adjust to the strangeness of the Eskimo camp.

Meanwhile, a relay of women kept bringing iron kettles full of tea. This tea, supplied by Peetyuk, was the first the Eskimos had tasted in over a year. Tea is the one luxury which Eskimos love above all others and that evening the assembled crowd must have drunk ten gallons of it.

Occasionally Peetyuk turned to his companions and explained something of what was being said.

Much of the talk concerned what had happened to individuals that winter; but there was general talk about the decrease in the number of deer, about the near-starvation winter just finished, and about the "old days" in the Barrens.

"Long time ago," Peetyuk told his friends, "Ihalmiut live more north at big lake called Angikuni. Those times, many more Eskimos. Have great camp there, maybe fifty tents. When Kakut little boy, white man come down river in canoe and big sickness come to that camp. Most people die . . ."

Here he was interrupted by some of the Eskimos. For a time he had no further chance to talk to his friends. Finally there came a pause in the spate of conversation.

"Have party now," he told them. "Eskimo party. Big fun. You watch!"

It was growing dark outside and one of the women began lighting a number of soapstone lamps, shallow stone dishes filled with rendered deer fat. The wicks were twists of the silky blooms of cotton grass, which grows everywhere on the arctic plains. The lamps burned with a clear, bright flame, lighting up the circle of dark, smiling faces which now almost filled the tent.

Old Kakut now produced a wooden hoop about three feet in diameter, over which a piece of caribou membrane had been tightly stretched.

A murmur of anticipation greeted the appearance of this drum and the Eskimos began to crowd back against the walls of the tent leaving a clear space in the center. The tent was growing hazy with tobacco smoke, for Peetyuk had distributed plugs of tobacco to all the men and women, and they had begun to light up tiny soapstone pipes.

Kakut shuffled into the middle of the tent looking even more like an amiable bear in his fur trousers and parka. Holding the drum in his left hand he began to twirl it, at the same time striking the rim with a stick held in his right hand. When the tempo had been set he bent over the drum and began to sing, while shuffling his feet in time to the music.

It was a weird, high-pitched song consisting of many short verses, after each of which the whole assembly joined in the chorus, wailing *"Ai-ya-ya-ya-yai, ai-ya-ya, ai-yai-a-ya . . ."*

It was so strange that at first Jamie could feel his back hair begin to prickle. However, after a while the rhythm of the drum began to affect him and he even found himself joining the chorus. He noticed that Awasin and Angeline were watching Kakut intently, and that they too were singing the refrain.

When the song ended, Kakut handed the drum to another man who also sang a song. So it went until all the men had done a turn. Between songs the tea went down at an alarming rate. Tobacco smoke rolled up thicker and thicker until one of the women lifted a side wall of the tent to let in some air, revealing a solid row of children lying on their tummies listening to their elders.

There came a pause in the singing and Peetyuk turned to his guests. "Now," he said sternly, "your turn. Make music for Eskimo."

"Oh no! Not me!" Jamie cried, but Awasin made no demur. Gravely the Indian boy got to his feet, stepped into the center of the tent and began to sing. It was a song Jamie had never heard before. It was wild and barbaric and it too had a wailing unearthly quality that seemed to speak of other ages, other races of mankind.

The Eskimos listened in dead silence, but when Awasin was done they shouted wildly and enthusiastically, even though they had not understood a word of it. They had no need to know the words; the music spoke to them of things they understood — of the immensity of the northern wilderness, of strange beings white men do not know, of tragedy and happiness, of love and death.

"What *was* that song?" Jamie asked urgently when Awasin rejoined him. "I never heard any Cree sing a song like that before."

Awasin smiled in some embarrassment. "An old song of the old people, Jamie. We do not sing such songs to white men, for they do not understand. They only hold their ears, and sometimes they laugh. But these people — they understand."

Jamie was hurt that he should have been considered too dull to understand, and when Peetyuk again insisted that he must do his part, he got to his feet and scrambled shyly into the center of the tent.

All eyes were on him as he took a deep breath, pinched his nose between finger and thumb of one hand, and clutched at his windpipe with the other hand.

Then the silence was broken by a sound as eerie as anything which had preceded it. A shrill, quavering whine filled the tent. The Eskimos sat as if petrified while from the darkness outside the lugubrious howling of sled dogs rose and fell almost in unison with the outlandish music Jamie was producing.

At last Jamie's hands fell to his sides and he went back to his place. The silence was complete. For a long minute no one even coughed. Then Peetyuk gave a great shout of applause and the rest of the Eskimos joined in.

"What was *that* noise?" Awasin cried in Jamie's ear. "You even frightened me! I never knew white men could make a noise like that!"

Jamie grinned, well satisfied with the effect his solo had produced.

"You Crees and Eskimos aren't the only ones can make wild songs," he explained proudly. "That was the bag-pipes. Or at least it was an imitation of them. My father taught me how to do it when I was just a kid. I never did it in front of you before, because, well, because I thought *you'd* laugh at *me!*"

Jamie's bagpipe imitation was the hit of the evening. Several Eskimo men began pounding him on the back, all talking at once. Peetyuk interjected with a demand that Jamie give an encore. It was a command performance.

Jamie obliged with "The Pibroch of Donal Dhu," and then "The Flowers of the Forest." He desisted only when he became so hoarse he could not go on.

When he finally sat down one of the women gave him a big mug of tea, and Peetyuk shook his white friend's arm and said, "Jamie, you are Inuk — an Eskimo. All people say you best singer in our country. Maybe you marry Eskimo girl and stay here, eh? Make very famous man!"

Whatever reservations and tensions the three strangers felt when they arrived had now completely dissolved. Even Angeline, who had been very silent, watching everything with careful eyes, had relaxed. She was now sitting beside an Eskimo girl of her own age, the two of them fingering and comparing each other's clothing, although they did not have a word in common. Occasionally she glanced at Peetyuk, half shyly and half proudly, for she was thinking to herself how much a man he seemed now that he was with his own people. Once Peetyuk caught her glance and returned it with a broad smile of delight, and Angeline felt very happy and content.

Well before midnight the visitors had begun to feel sleepy. But the party was not yet over. One by one the Eskimo women, and finally even the children, took the drum and sang their own songs. Kettles and trays of boiled and roasted deer meat began to appear. The tea continued to flow like a running river. Some of the women and men began making cat's cradles — string figures — with their fingers.

Eventually Jamie could keep his eyes open no longer. He began to drowse, and Kakut, seeing this, spoke up in his gruff voice. The hubbub ceased. People began to file quietly out of the tent and it was soon empty except for the four travelers, Kakut, his wife, and their grown son Bellikari.

"Now we sleep," Peetyuk said to his friends. "All sleep at back of tent under *tuktu* robes."

Too sleepy to be bothered by the lack of privacy, Jamie and Awasin shrugged off their outer clothing and crawled in. Peetyuk followed, then Kakut and Bellikari. Angeline and the Eskimo woman snuggled into their own corner of the communal bed. The last fat lamp flickered and went out and there was silence in the camp of the Ihalmiut.

CHAPTER 10

Innuit Ku

Exhausted by the trek north-
ward and by the late night, the boys and Angeline slept so
soundly they did not waken until the morning was well
along. When they came crawling sleepily out from under
the robes it was to find the big tent deserted. Pulling on
their clothing, they went outside.

The scene which met their eyes was one of monumental
confusion. People were running about in all directions,
carrying loads here and there, dragging dogs toward sleds,
shouting, laughing, and generally getting in one another's
way. Children raced around amongst the older people,
pursuing fleeing dogs. Where five tents had stood the
night before now there was only Kakut's. The rest were
reduced to bundles of sticks and mounds of deer hides.

"What on earth's happening?" Jamie asked Peetyuk.

"We go my mother's camp today," Peetyuk explained.
"All people come along. Time to leave small camps, go Innuit Ku for big camp. Soon ice gone then deer not able
walk all over plains. Must cross rivers at narrow places.
People go there, make big hunt with kayaks."

Kakut joined them, and at his gesture they followed to

where his wife was tending a small fire of moss and twigs.
A big iron kettle hung over it, simmering and hissing. The
Eskimo woman smiled a greeting, then dipped out chunks
of boiled meat which she handed to them without benefit
of plates. The meat was hot, and Jamie was soon juggling
his piece from hand to hand.

"This is what I call a breakfast on the run," he mumbled
as he burned his lips on the meat. "But good, mind you,"
he hastened to add as Peetyuk threw him a sharp look.

Awasin grinned. "You were not so fussy last winter
when we lived at Hidden Valley. I think you ate your
breakfast with your fingers there — and raw sometimes."

"I could get our tin plates from the cariole," Angeline
suggested.

"No, sister," Awasin told her. "These people do not use
plates. We should not make them feel the lack by using
ours."

Breakfast did not take long, and soon the boys were
wandering about the camp with Peetyuk as their guide.
They looked with keen interest at the dogs: magnificent
big beasts which were nearly twice the size of woodland
huskies, and strikingly patterned in black and white.
Awasin was curious to know why the Eskimos did not
keep their dogs tied when not in use. He also commented
on their good nature.

"That why we not tie," Peetyuk explained. "If *you* are
dog tied up all time, *you* get mean. Eskimo dog free like
Eskimo. So he be happy like Eskimo."

The boys also admired the sleds, which although built
like Peetyuk's were much larger. Kakut's sled was twenty

feet long, composed of two massive runners joined by a dozen short cross-pieces lashed across the top. Jamie whistled when he saw the size of this sled and the enormous load which had been piled on it. He was frankly skeptical that it could ever be moved by dog power, but his skepticism vanished when Kakut and Bellikari hitched up their team of eighteen dogs. These were not hitched one behind the other in forest style. Each was on a separate trace so that the whole team could spread out fanlike ahead of the sled.

The last thing to go on Kakut's sled (his tent had already been pulled down and packed by Bellikari and his mother) was a strange-looking object some fifteen feet in length. It consisted of an open latticework of very small curved willow ribs, fastened with rawhide to a number of long stringers of thin spruce. It looked like the skeleton of some gigantic fish.

"Kayak," Peetyuk explained as he noticed Awasin's interest. "When we come Innuit Ku, Kakut get deer hides and cover kayak. Then float very good."

A shout from Kakut drew everyone's attention. His big sled now stood ready to go and one by one the other Eskimo men drove their sleds over to join him. Old women and young children sat on top of the loads, but the younger women and older children (packing bundles on their backs) prepared to walk alongside. Some of them had hung pack-saddles on half-grown dogs which were still too young to work in the sled teams. Some young dogs were towing miniature *travois* consisting of two long poles stretching out behind, on which a small platform bearing

a light load had been lashed. Five or six even younger
dogs — hardly more than puppies — frolicked free
amongst the sleds and people.

It was a gay scene, but with a wild and ancient look
about it. The mob of fur-clad people, the howling dogs,
the great sweep of rolling tundra under a white spring sky
were things which had not changed through many centuries, perhaps not for many millennia.

The boys and Angeline, with their teams, joined Kakut.
The old man gave the signal to move off by cracking an
immensely long whip over his dogs' heads. In a moment
the whole cavalcade was moving.

Progress was slow, for there was already much open
ground. The sleds moved at the pace of the walking
women and children; but no one seemed concerned. There
was much joking back and forth, and when one of the
younger men, attempting to show off his dog-driving skill,
incautiously drove over a piece of bad ice and plunged
through to his neck, the whole assemblage stopped to
howl and rock with merriment. It was laughter in which
the victim himself was quick to join, once he had scrambled back onto firm ice and changed into dry clothing.

The destination was only eight miles away, but it was
nearly dusk before the caravan reached Kakut Lake and
came in sight of the tents of a camp. Everyone in this new
camp was out on the ice to greet the visitors. Once more
Jamie, Awasin and Angeline had to go through the wel-
coming ceremony, including another gigantic meal, which
this time was served in the tent of Epeetna, Peetyuk's
mother.

Epeetna was still a young woman and good-looking, if somewhat plump. She lived with her married brother Ohoto — Peetyuk's uncle — who was a powerfully built, stocky man in his mid-thirties. When Ohoto saw Peetyuk he caught him in a bear-hug, lifted him clean off the ground, and carried the red-head, yelling and kicking, up to his mother's tent where Epeetna greeted her son with a rub of noses and much back-patting.

Kakut's group pitched no tents but simply moved in with friends in the new camp. This led to some crowding, since there were nearly forty men, women and children all told and only four tents. But no one seemed to mind, and there was another late party that night with the whole population crowded into a single tent. Despite their desire not to offend anyone, this was too much for Awasin, Jamie and Angeline and they managed to sneak away to their carioles, where they were preparing to get out their sleeping robes when Peetyuk and Ohoto descended on them.

"What you do?" Peetyuk cried indignantly. "My mother think you not like. Go very sad. All Eskimos go sad. Come back to tent, eh?"

Awasin and Jamie exchanged glances. Jamie shrugged. "Nothing else for it, chum," he whispered. Then: "We just came down to get our robes, Peetyuk. We were coming right back."

Peetyuk snorted. "Robes! No need robes. Plenty people on sleeping bench, keep everybody warm!"

"Uh-huh; that's what I was afraid of," Jamie muttered, but Peetyuk did not hear him.

It was a night Jamie long remembered. There were nine

people on the sleeping ledge. The snores, grunts, groans and whistles would have done credit to a boiler factory. Not only that, but several of the Eskimos were almost as athletic when asleep as when awake. Feet in his ribs, elbows in his ear, and once a large hand over his mouth kept Jamie from being bored. Angeline fared a little better for the women were quieter sleepers, but even she looked weary and hollow-eyed when morning finally freed them from the communal bed.

Once again they were treated to the sight of a camp being broken, since the Kakut Lake families had decided to join the rest in the trek to the Kazon River.

"We gather people like a snowball rolling downhill," was Jamie's comment to Awasin and Angeline.

Angeline looked very thoughtful. "That is so, Jamie. I wonder how many will there be in bed tonight?"

"I hate to think!" said Jamie, shuddering.

But they were lucky. The next camp was at the north end of Kakut Lake, and when they reached it they found it had been broken up the day before and its people had gone on. Consequently, everyone slept out that night, and even Peetyuk seemed grateful for fresh air and space, and for the privacy of his own robes.

Just before noon the following morning the straggling line of sleds and people crossed the strip of land beyond Kakut Lake and reached the high cutbanks of Innuit Ku. To Jamie and Awasin the moment was one of some solemnity, for this was their return to the big river which the previous year had carried them north to the great adventure of their lives.

Innuit Ku was not as they had seen it last. It was ice-covered now, but the thaw waters had broken the ice loose from shore and had risen under it until the huge cakes were cracking and splitting and almost pushing over the edge of the banks. From beneath this uneasy layer of ice came a deep-throated roar of barely contained waters.

"That ice will go out anytime," Awasin said in awe. "I do not want to be on it when it goes!"

But there was no question of traveling on the river, and Kakut led his procession north along the eastern bank. About noon he called a halt and everyone scattered to gather fuel for a tea fire.

Jamie and Awasin went inland to collect willows, leaving Angeline and Peetyuk to get out the grub. Suddenly they felt the frozen ground tremble under their feet. At the same instant there came a dull, reverberating roar, and even as they looked at each other with startled eyes it rose to a tremendous clashing thunder.

"The river!" Awasin yelled, and the two boys turned and ran toward the travel camp.

They arrived in time to watch a fearsome spectacle. The flood waters building up along hundreds of miles of lakes and rivers were throwing off their chains. The whole surface of the river was in agony. Gigantic cakes of ice lifted, twisted, slipped and crashed as they began to tear apart and move shudderingly downstream. Then, from upstream, a wall of ice and water fifteen or twenty feet high appeared and came roaring down toward the watchers.

Clutching Angeline against him, Awasin watched wide-eyed as the mighty battering-ram of ice and water swept down toward them. Jamie's lips moved as he shouted something, but nothing could be heard above the cataclysmic crash of ice and rocks and water. The flood wave came abreast of them and they saw blocks of ice ten feet in thickness flung high into the air to fall in great gouts of spray and shattered ice. Ice crystals glittered and shimmered above.the unleashed power of the raging river like a jeweled fog.

No one moved during the half hour that it took for the flood to subside a little. When at last Kakut called on them to make their fires and to eat their meal, even the Eskimos went about their business in a subdued silence.

"Winter dead," Peetyuk said as the four sat drinking their tea. "Now good time for Eskimo people begin. Look. *Tingmea* come now!" He pointed to the sky where a long, ragged "V" of geese was following the course of the river northward.

The cavalcade continued to make slow progress. Much open rock and thawing bog had appeared from under the receding snows, and the dogs were hard put to haul the sleds along. Often they had to be helped by shouting Eskimos who grabbed the traces and pulled as hard as the dogs themselves. It was late afternoon before they came in sight of a cluster of tents pitched on the east shore of a lakelike expansion of Innuit Ku.

This was the site of the central summer camp. Here the Ihalmiut usually gathered to intercept the buck caribou who traveled north some days after the passing of the does. With the arrival of Kakut's cavalcade there were twelve families of Eskimos, totaling about sixty people in all. These were the last survivors of what had once been a great population spread far and wide across the northern plains.

These were the people of Innuit Ku, the River of Men, which had once known their camps along more than four hundred miles of its sinuous length. They were the last of the People, for the River of Men had become the River of Ghosts, and the mighty land was almost empty of mankind.

CHAPTER 11

Elaitutna

During the next few weeks the boys and Angeline remained at the Eskimo camp. Although the rivers had broken up, they were still full of floating ice and could not yet be used as canoe routes. The spring thaw, which comes so swiftly to the arctic plains, had turned the country into a morass of melting snow, swollen lakelets and sodden muskeg, so that overland travel was also out of the question for the time being.

Although the travelers were impatient to reach the Viking cache, they did not find the enforced delay difficult to endure. Life with the Eskimos was full of interest.

Jamie and the two young Crees soon felt at home amongst the Ihalmiut, but all the same they insisted on erecting their own tent. Eskimo hospitality, as they had found, was apt to be a little overwhelming. However, they ate many of their meals with the people, and they were in great demand as guests.

The Eskimo diet consisted almost entirely of deer meat, cooked in a variety of ways and sometimes eaten raw. During the first days of the visit, deer meat was in short supply, since without ammunition the Eskimos had not been able to kill many of the migrating does. However, on the second day at the Innuit Ku camp, Peetyuk led Jamie and Awasin off on a hunting expedition, and when they returned late that day, having killed six fat deer, they were greeted as mighty hunters. These deer were particularly welcome since the Eskimo men were anxious to get their kayaks covered in preparation for the arrival of the bucks and good deer hides were scarce.

Jamie and Awasin watched with keen interest as Kakut prepared his kayak. First he soaked the fresh hides in the river for two days, then he scraped both sides, removing the hair and the fat. The resulting parchmentlike skins were moistened again and carefully stretched over the skeleton of the kayak, and the hides were stitched tightly together by three women. This stitching, done with sinew and bone needles, was so fine that the finished seams were completely waterproof.

As the skins dried they shrank, so that the kayak covering was stretched as tightly as a drumhead.

One morning Kakut decided to test his kayak. He picked it up easily — for it weighed almost nothing — carried it to the edge of the lake and laid it carefully on the water, where it floated as high and as light as a pinch of thistledown. Wading out alongside it, Kakut nimbly swung himself into the tiny cockpit, picked up his long double-bladed paddle, and shot off over the lake.

It looked easy, and when Peetyuk slyly intimated to Awasin that *only* an Eskimo could handle a kayak, Awasin incautiously took up the challenge and agreed to try his skill.

Peetyuk quietly spread the word around the camp, and when Awasin went down to the shore he discovered to his dismay that almost all the Eskimos had gathered to watch him. Trying to ignore the expectant mob, he launched the kayak and, having drawn on a pair of skin boots — *kamik-pak* — which came above his knees and were quite waterproof, he waded out.

Getting into the kayak proved harder than it looked. On his first attempt he tipped the little craft over on its side and half filled it. Grimly he hauled it ashore, emptied it, and prepared to try again. This time, by dint of jumping into the cockpit rather than attempting to step into it, he managed to get aboard. Instantly the kayak tipped to the left, almost spilling him out.

Jamie, Peetyuk and the Eskimos were vastly entertained. Shouts of laughter and of good-natured advice rained down on poor Awasin as he fought to get the skittish little boat under control. Finally he got it balanced and took a stroke with the paddle. The kayak shot ahead so fast that Awasin's mouth fell open in surprise, and the watchers on shore almost convulsed themselves with mirth. Once under way, Awasin seemed unable to stop. The kayak leaped out over the icy waters of the lake with Awasin paddling for dear life as he tried to turn for shore again. Having described a huge and erratic circle, he eventually got the long, pointed bow headed for the land. But as he approached the shore he attempted to slow down by backwatering too strongly with one end of the paddle. Before he could as much as change his grip the kayak tipped right over and Awasin disappeared from view. A moment later his head popped to the surface and he began dog-paddling for shore. He had not gone a yard, however, when a look of blank surprise came over his face. His struggles ceased and he rose slowly to his feet, for the water was hardly more than knee deep.

Peetyuk could not contain himself. Choking with laughter, he rolled on the gravelly shore until Awasin, stumbling over unseen rocks, came charging up the beach, grabbed Peetyuk by one leg, and hauled him into the lake. Helpless with laughter, Peetyuk could put up no resistance. His head disappeared under the surface, and when he came up again, spouting water like a whale, the Eskimos lost all control and the shrieks of mirth became earsplitting.

The kayak was rescued and dried out, and then Jamie was offered a chance to show what *he* could do. He declined, firmly but politely, while secretly making up his mind that the only way they would ever get *him* into the flimsy craft would be to hog-tie him first.

One day about a week after their arrival at the summer camp, Ohoto (who had been making daily excursions on foot toward the south) returned to camp in a great state of excitement. He brought the news that the long-awaited herds of bucks were coming.

The six kayaks which had been readied for use were hurriedly carried over a ridge behind the camp to the banks of the small but swift river which flowed into Innuit Ku from the northeast. Here they were concealed in a clump of willows. Beside each kayak an Eskimo hunter lay down in hiding.

Two other men went loping across country to the east where a long row of *inukok,* spaced about fifty feet apart, had been built for nearly a mile in a diagonal line toward the southeast. The two men ran from stoneman to stoneman, crowning each with a big lump of muskeg from which dried grasses waved. The addition of these "heads" gave the stonemen a resemblance to crouching human beings. This was a "deer fence," and its function was to deflect the approaching herds toward the particular crossing place on the river near which the hunters and kayaks lay hidden.

Back at camp the women and children were busy rounding up the dogs and tying them securely so they would not rush out and alarm the caribou. All fires were put out and the ashes damped with water so the deer would not catch the smell of smoke.

When everything was ready those Eskimos who were not otherwise engaged climbed the slope of the ridge near camp and took up vantage points from which they could observe the hunt.

Peetyuk, Awasin, Jamie and Angeline took up a position at the north end of the ridge, almost directly above the chosen crossing place.

Old Kakut was at the south end, searching the southern horizon with an ancient brass telescope. At last he laid down the tube and began waving his arms up and down.

Another man, stationed not far from Jamie, repeated the signal so that the hidden hunters by the kayaks could see it.

"They come now," Peetyuk muttered to his friends.

Straining their eyes, the watchers could just make out a blob of movement on the slopes of a hill two miles away to the south. As they watched, it began to resolve itself into a familiar pattern. Long skeins of caribou twisted slowly down the slope and headed out along the floor of the valley leading past the ridge. These were all bucks and they were in no hurry. They seemed to drift aimlessly before a light southerly wind, often stopping to browse on reindeer moss which had been exposed by the melting snows.

They moved unbearably slowly — or so it seemed to the watchers. Finally the lead bucks reached the stoneman fence. Although they did not seem much frightened by it, they nevertheless swung away towards the northwest.

Two hours after they had first appeared in view the lead bucks reached the riverbank. Here they milled about for another twenty minutes, apparently undecided whether or not to cross the swift stretch of water. Then the pressure of the herds building up behind made up their minds for them and a bunch of fifty or sixty animals plunged into the stream. With heads held high, they struck out buoyantly for the opposite shore.

Jamie's gaze was glued to the barely discernible shapes of the kayakers, but they remained motionless.

"What's the matter?" he whispered to Peetyuk. "Why don't they launch the kayaks? Those deer are pretty near across!"

"Wait," Peetyuk calmed him. "Watch close, you see."

Having crossed safely, the first deer shook themselves like dogs and began to move on north. Now a herd of perhaps a hundred which had been watching them from the south shore seemed to conclude that the crossing was a good one, and they too plunged into the fast-moving current.

They were halfway over when the six hunters leaped to their feet, seized their kayaks, flung them into the stream and jumped aboard. Whipping the water with their paddles, they shot down on the startled deer and in a few seconds had cut them off from both banks.

The caribou whirled in panic, swimming upstream and circling so tightly that they got in each other's way, which increased their panic. In the meantime each kayaker, while handling his light craft with one hand, pulled a short spear from its lashings on the foredeck. Wielding these three-foot lances tipped with broad triangular steel blades, the hunters closed in on the milling animals.

One quick thrust into the back of each swimming buck just behind the ribcage was enough. Then the hunter maneuvered his kayak within reach of another deer. Soon the cold green waters of the river were darkening and becoming turbid with blood. A score of dead and dying deer were drifting swiftly downstream from the killing place. The survivors scrambled ashore wherever they could, and made off at an ungainly gallop across the plains.

The whole incident, from the time the hunters appeared until the deer fled, had taken no more than five minutes. As Jamie, Awasin and Angeline got stiffly to their feet

along with the Eskimos and began to make their way down the hill to the crossing place, the two men who had gone off to repair the *inukok* appeared away downstream. Each of them had a long pole with a hook on it, and they were busy hauling the floating carcasses to shore.

"Your people don't *need* rifles," Jamie told Peetyuk admiringly. "That was the slickest hunt I ever saw."

Peetyuk grinned. "They hunt good, but not all time can catch deer at river. Then come hungry times, if have no bullets for guns. Come on. Now we have big feed of marrowbones."

There was a gigantic celebration in the camp that night. Everyone stuffed himself on the sweet white marrow from

the long bones of the bucks and on other delicacies such as roast kidney, hearts, and whole broiled briskets dripping with fat. When the eating had eased off a little (it never ceased entirely), the drums came out and there were songs and dancing.

One of the dancers was an ancient old man whose face was so lined and creased it looked like a piece of corrugated cardboard. Yet despite his age he was very agile, and when he sang and danced everyone stopped to watch and listen.

"Who's that old fellow?" Jamie asked Peetyuk.

"He Elaitutna. Most old man of Ihalmiut. He *angeokok*, big magic maker. He speak to many spirits, and he know many story. Tomorrow, maybe, he tell you some."

The next afternoon Peetyuk took his friends to visit Elaitutna. The old man did not rise from his pile of robes when they entered his tent, but only nodded and looked sharply at them with tiny, jet-black eyes which were almost hidden under folds of wrinkled skin. After a time he spoke briefly to Peetyuk, and Peetyuk replied at considerable length before explaining the conversation to his friends.

"He ask what you do in our land. I tell him about Viking cache and say we come to get. He not like that. Maybe he try stop us. He think Viking cache some kind of magic. Wait now, I try find out."

Peetyuk spoke again in Eskimo, and the old man nodded his head but said nothing. It seemed like an impasse until Jamie had an inspiration. He had several plugs of tobacco in his pocket, intended as gifts for some of the hunters. He pulled out three plugs and gravely offered them to the old man.

Elaitutna's clawlike hand came out with the speed of a striking snake, seized the plugs, and plunged them under his loose parka. He looked shrewdly at Jamie for a moment, then he seemed to make up his mind. Rising to his knees he began to rummage about under the sleeping platform and at last he drew out a strange contraption made of wood and bone. He held it up so they could see it, but only Jamie recognized it.

"That's a crossbow," he said in surprise. "Eskimos don't use crossbows! They were something Europeans used hundreds of years ago. Where did he get it, Peetyuk?"

"He say he made it," Peetyuk replied after translating

the question. "He say Innuit find how to make from men called Inohowik — Men of Iron — who come to land long, long ago. Elaitutna say he tell story, if we want."

"It may be something to do with the Vikings," Jamie answered, his voice rising with excitement. "Ask him to tell the story, Peetyuk. Ask him, please!"

Peetyuk turned back to the old man and repeated the request. Elaitutna raised his eyes so that he was looking past the boys. He seemed to be peering through the wall of the tent into some limitless distance they could not penetrate. For a long time he was motionless. Then his voice broke the waiting silence.

CHAPTER 12

The Viking Bow

"THIS BOW WAS A MAN'S WEAPON! It gave my people strength for more generations than I can count. It was the gift we laid aside when the white men brought rifles to our land. That was a wrong thing we did, for men should not lay down the gifts which make them great.

"This was a gift that came to us in time out of memory; but *I* have that memory, for I am *angeokok,* a man of magic things, and the memory lived through all the many winters until it came to me.

"This was a gift of the Inohowik. They were mighty beings, more than men and yet not gods, for death felled them in the end. They were pale-skinned and bearded. Their eyes were blue with the color of deep ice.

"As for the place they came from, who knows their lands? We only knew it lay far to the east, over the salt water that has no shore. They traveled over that water in boats fifty times the size of a kayak, so it was said.

"In those days we lived closer to the salt water and there were not many of us in the land, but the Itkilit — the Indians — were many. They hated us and hunted us

like rabbits. It was their custom to come far out into the
plains in summertime, and they would fall upon the Innuit
camps and slaughter all within. So we were much afraid.

"In the hunter's moon of a certain year our people were
camped on a river called Ikarluku. One morning a boy
went to the river to spear fish, but soon he came running
back crying that the Itkilit were come. The men seized
their spears and stood trembling in front of the tents. But
it was not the feared Itkilit who came down the river — it
was a strange canoe made of heavy wood and rowed by
eight strange men.

"These were Inohowik. They sat in pairs, and a ninth
stood and faced them from the stern. He wore a shining
iron cap upon his head and iron sheets that caught the
rising sun upon his chest.

"The Innuit were afraid, for they thought these must be
devils. They watched in terror as the Inohowik came to

shore. The tall one, he who stood in the stern, landed first. He held up a huge round shield ahead of him, and it was painted white as snow. Then he flung down the shield and on it laid a mighty iron knife as long as a man's leg. So he stood with empty hands, and the people saw he had come to them without the black blood of evil in his heart.

"This was the coming of the Inohowik. They could not speak our tongue, nor we speak theirs. Yet they made it known by signs that they had come many moons' travel, and wished now to return to a far distant place beyond the salt waters. After a time the People understood that the Inohowik had come to our shores in a great canoe and then had ventured south into the forests where Itkilit bands came on them at night and slew all but these nine. The nine fled to the north again, but when at last they reached the salt water shores they found their great canoe had gone, and they were left alone.

"They were hungry when they came to the Innuit camps, and the People fed them, for that is our way. It was a day of days when they came amongst us. It was the beginning of our greatness.

"As to what happened afterwards — the stories tell of many things. They tell of the strength of the strangers, and of the tools and weapons they possessed. Much was of iron, which we had never seen before, and which we came to call by the name of one of the strangers — *howik*. But the leader was called Koonar.

"When they had been with the People a time, they began to ask if there was a way around the salt sea to the northward. When they were told there was no way, they were bitterly unhappy. Then the snows began, and they came into the houses of the People and began to live with them.

"For more than a year they lived with the people. They learned to hunt as the Innuit hunt. Most of them gave up their strange clothing and wore the fur clothing of the Innuit. But Koonar would not do this, and always wore his clothes of iron. Even in the hard heart of winter he wore his horned iron cap which made him look like a musk-ox bull.

"Koonar was a giant. He could carry the whole carcass of a caribou on his back. When he wielded his great iron knife he could split a caribou as easily as a woman splits a fish. Koonar lived with a man called Kiliktuk, who was *angeokok*. Kiliktuk had a daughter named Airut, and after a while Airut grew big with child, and the child was Koonar's. Then the Innuit were happy for they thought Koonar and his men would stay with them always. The Inohowik had much to teach the People. They taught them how to strike fire with iron and stone, how to build salmon weirs, how to read the stars so one could find one's way, and many other wonderful things. Yet for all their wisdom they were as children in our land, and it was we who taught them how to live in the country of the great plains.

"The next winter the Inohowik gathered in an igloo and talked a long time. Koonar was not with them, for he was in the igloo of Kiliktuk and Airut, and there he lived with the baby son which had been born to Airut. Then the eight came to him and said they would leave. They said they would march to the shores of the salt sea and then go south to the forests far enough to find the wood with which to build a great canoe, and so sail off into the east to their far distant home.

"They asked Koonar to go with them, for Koonar was their leader. Koonar said he would do this, although he did not feel pleasure in it.

"Then the People were angry. All of the Inohowik had taken wives amongst the people, and the Innuit were angry that these women should be deserted. Things might have come to trouble, but Koonar stopped it. He said if we would let his men travel south, he would remain behind with us forever, and he promised to teach us many secrets.

"So it was agreed. The People spoke against the journey all the same, for they knew the Inohowik would not survive. They knew that if the winter blizzards did not destroy them, then the Itkilit would. But the eight would not listen. One day they departed with dogs and sleds the Innuit had given them.

"They vanished into the drifting snow and were never seen again. Somewhere in the dark night they met the fury of the land and perished.

"And so the tale of the Inohowik becomes the tale of Koonar, and of Airut, and of the children she bore. Koonar was much loved amongst my people. Often he spoke of things he had known and seen in distant places. Much of what he said was beyond belief, for he told of great battles fought on land and sea, with such fierce weapons that men's blood flowed like the spring rains.

"The Innuit asked Koonar to show them how to make

such weapons, but he refused. He said he would not give the People the means to destroy themselves. He spoke so because he did not understand the Innuit. He did not understand that we do not take life unless we must. Koonar was afraid we would become like the Itkilit if he told us the secret of the killing weapons.

"The People loved Koonar, but he grew sad as the years passed. He would no longer go out hunting, but sat at his camp staring toward the east, and talking to himself in his strange tongue. The Innuit were sad for him, but they could not help him.

"One spring it was decided to move inland from Ikarluku to the rich caribou lands near the River of Men; for it was felt that with Koonar to help the People they would be able to defend themselves against the Itkilit.

"So the move was made. And it is said that when they marched to the westward, Koonar was the last of the marchers, and he turned many times toward the east, and that he wept.

"The People came to the banks of the River of Men and they made a camp not far from Angikuni Lake, and it was a good place, with many fat deer. For three years they prospered, and all thought this was because of Koonar's good luck, and they loved him even more.

"Then, in the fish-spearing moon of the third year, the men decided to go north down Innuit Ku in search of musk ox. They asked Koonar to go with them, but he said he was sick and could not go. But his was a sickness of the spirit, not of the flesh.

"So the hunters took their kayaks and went north, and

Koonar remained in the camp with the women and children and old people. And it happened that when the men
had been gone a while, a great party of Itkilit came down
the river and fell on the Innuit camp.

"Then there was a terrible slaughter. It is said that half
the women and children were slain. But *all* would have
been slain had it not been for Koonar.

"Koonar was a little way from the camp, sitting alone, as
was his habit. When he heard the screaming of women
and children he came running back. He had his great knife
in his hand, and his horned hat on his head, and his iron
shirt was shining in the sun.

"He came down upon the camp, bellowing like the great
brown bear of the Barrens. He ran straight at the Itkilit
and his great knife flashed and grew red, and it flashed red
many times.

"The Itkilit could not stand against him. He killed
many, but the rest fled to their canoes and turned south up
the river. But before they passed from sight, one of them
turned and fired an arrow from his long bow, and the arrow went below Koonar's iron shirt and pierced his belly.

"When the Innuit men came back to the camp they
found many of their wives and children buried beneath
rock graves, and the women weeping for them. Airut and
both of Koonar's children were amongst the dead. Koonar
lay in a tent and would speak to no one. He had drawn the
arrow out of his gut with his own hand, but the wound
was black and stinking.

"He would speak to none until Kiliktuk, the *angeokok*,
came to his side. First Koonar swore terrible oaths. Then

he bade Kiliktuk bring him wood and the hard, springy horns of musk ox. And when Kiliktuk had done these things, Koonar told him to shape the wood so, and the horn so, and join them so. And when it was done, Kiliktuk held in his hand just such a bow as this which I have shown to you.

"Then Koonar spoke. 'This is the Child of Death. Take it as my gift. Take it and go to the forests where the Itkilit are, and slay them where they walk and where they sleep. Let not one remain alive in all the land.'

"And when he had spoken, he died.

"Kiliktuk had his body carried to a certain high place beside Innuit Ku, and there he was laid with all the things which had been his, yes, even to his great knife which was a priceless thing. And when this had been done, the People built a house over Koonar, and they built it of stone as he had told them the houses were built in his own land.

"There Koonar lies. And Koonar's House is the place that you have seen.

"As for the bow. We did not take it south in search of vengeance. That is not our way. But we made many such bows, and then we were able to kill deer whenever there was need of meat. And with these bows we were able to keep the Itkilit out of our lands, for they grew to have a terrible fear of the Child of Death.

"So we prospered until the Innuit were as many as flies over all this land. We used the Child of Death to make life, and it was good. It was the greatest gift that ever came to us, and had we kept it, who knows, perhaps we would still be many, and not a people numbering so few it will not be many more winters before the last of us has vanished.

"Now I am tired; I am old and soon must sleep. Go now, for I am old. . . ."

CHAPTER 13

A Change of Plan

ANGELINE AND THE THREE BOYS were engrossed in their own thoughts as they left Elaitutna's tent and made their way back to their own place. The Cree girl's eyes were shining with the sheen of suppressed tears. The tragic tale of Koonar seemed so vivid to her that it might have been something which had happened only yesterday.

They had all been deeply moved by the story, but its effect on Peetyuk was particularly profound. He remained silent, and his usually cheerful face was clouded with inner misery. By suppertime the other three had begun to worry about him, and they tried to cheer him up.

"It was a long time ago Koonar died," Awasin reminded him.

Peetyuk raised his face, and his eyes seemed peculiarly dark and brooding.

"I not think of Koonar. I think of the Ihalmiut. They *my* people. When I grow up here, I know often there no meat, and sometimes babies die and old people starve. Now I think what Elaitutna say. One time many people, many deer, and no people starve. Now few people, few deer, and

maybe soon all people starve. I think this happen to Ihalmiut if no one help."

"That's the Government's job, to help when people
starve," Jamie said. "The trouble is, nobody but a couple
of traders knows about your people, Peetyuk. I bet the
Government doesn't even know they exist. But when we
go south we'll tell everybody about them, and about
what's happening to them."

Awasin's quiet voice ruthlessly punctured Jamie's enthusiasm.

"Do you think they will listen, Jamie? Do not forget
what happened to the Chipeweyans. Many times the
white men have been asked for help, but how often has
help come? Peetyuk's people are far away from your people. Even if the white men believe us, they will find it easy
to forget."

"But I won't *let* them forget!" Jamie cried defensively.
"I'll see they don't. I'll make such a stink everyone will
hear about it and they'll *have* to do something!"

Awasin was inexorable. "How will you do that? You are
only one person and the police are hunting you. Who will
listen to your voice? I know how Peetyuk feels, Jamie, but
you can never know. You are my best friend, and a friend
of the Indians and the Eskimos, but you can never know
what we feel. We will get little help from the white men."

Jamie was struck silent by an unfamiliar strain of bitter-
ness in Awasin's voice. Before he could think of a reply,
Peetyuk broke in.

"Awasin say truth. I tell how it was with Ihalmiut. You
listen good, Jamie. One time Ihalmiut strong, get plenty

deer meat, hunt white fox all winter. Every two winters, strongest men take big load white fox to coast to trader. Bring back guns, shells, fox traps. Very long, hard trip, take two-three months. Only men with full bellies can make such trip. Only hunter with full belly can go hundred miles on Barrens in winter for catch white fox. Then many years ago, when I not yet born, men take big load white fox to trader. When they get to coast, trader say white fox no good now. Not worth nothing. Men come back without guns and shells. That winter ten-twenty people die because men have no bullets to kill deer in wintertime. After that, cannot hunt fox in winter. And every year not so many deer. Too much kill by white men in the south. So Eskimos must stay at camp and eat little, and everyone hungry before spring come. Four-five years ago Ohoto and three men go coast again. Tell trader must have shells. He laugh and say, bring many furs.

"Awasin right. White men only help white men. My father white man, but maybe I try forget that. Better my father Eskimo."

For the first time since he had come to the north, Jamie was aware of the chasm yawning between him and the people of that land. The sensation frightened him.

"Listen," he said desperately. "Not all whites are like the ones you've had to deal with. What about my Uncle Angus? And there are lots more like him down south. I tell you, if they only knew what was happening they'd send help. We'll *make* the Government do something. . . ." His voice trailed off lamely, for he could see that Awasin and Peetyuk did not believe him. He felt utterly miserable,

and very lonely. He was wracking his brain for some way
to heal the breach when Angeline spoke. Her voice was
gentle.

"I have been thinking. Jamie has said the Viking things
are worth much money to the people in the south. Those
were Koonar's things. He married an Eskimo woman and
had children here. Would he not have wished to help the
Eskimos even more than he did? Do you not think, if those
things are worth much money, that some of it should go to
Peetyuk's people? Then they could buy guns and shells
and other things they must have to live."

Jamie's relief was almost pathetic.

"Sure!" he cried. "That's it! I tell you, that stuff's worth
thousands to a museum. There'll be plenty of money to
look after Uncle Angus and all Peetyuk's people too. And
listen, another thing, newspapers will want to hear the
story of how we found the stuff. We can tell them all
about the Eskimos' troubles. It'll get read all over the
country. The Government will be bound to step in. They
won't be *able* to forget about it."

Peetyuk was looking at Angeline, and for the first time
that evening a smile flickered on his face. He half reached
out his hand as if to touch her shoulder, then thought better of it and turned, not to Jamie, but to Awasin.

"You think that work, Awasin?"

"Perhaps," Awasin replied cautiously. "*If* we *can* sell
these things ourselves. But the white men might take them
from us and give nothing back. Such things have happened with our people — and with yours."

"It won't happen *this* time!" Jamie cut in fiercely. "We

found the stuff and nobody can take it away from us. We'll cache it before we get to The Pas and just take one thing to show what we've got. And we won't let anyone know where the cache is until we're sure they're going to play square."

"That is a good plan," Awasin agreed. "Only I do not like going to The Pas. There we have no friends, and some enemies. The police there must be very angry with us. They will not make it easy for us."

An idea struck Jamie and came bubbling out of him like a waterfall.

"Peetyuk! When your people used to go to the coast, where did they go? Was it to Churchill? Could we go out the same way? If we could get to Churchill we'd be all set. It's a pretty big place and nobody would know who we are. I could wire my old school principal in Toronto from there. He was a great bug on history. He knows the museum people. I'll bet he'd help us all he could."

Peetyuk tried to deal with this spate of questions.

"Old times my people go in winter, across country, with dogsled to Churchill. Not go straight way because might meet Chipeweyans. Go long way round down Angiku — Big River — nearly to coast. Our people call Churchill Iglu-ujarik — Stone House — because big stone fort there. I not know for sure, but think maybe we go down Big River with canoe."

The depression which had been the aftermath of the visit to Elaitutna had now been dispelled. There was an excited babble of talk as the four began discussing details of the changed plans. It was interrupted when Peetyuk's

Uncle Ohoto lifted the tent flap and thrust in his round, beaming face to announce that supper was ready at his tent.

They trooped after him to his *topay* and found places on the floor around the big wooden meat tray which Peetyuk's mother had filled to overflowing with boiled ribs. As they ate, Peetyuk explained the new plans to the several Eskimos present.

Kakut, who had joined them for the meal, listened intently. "*Eema!*" he said thoughtfully. "In the very old days the people sometimes went down Big River in kayaks to salt water and there met the sea Innuit to trade for seal skins. But none of *us* has ever gone that way in summer — only in winter, on the ice. We will ask Elaitutna about it. He is the one who knows about the old things."

During the next few days the spring thaw was almost brought to a standstill by the return of bad weather. Frost at night, and gray, windy days with frequent sleet squalls kept the river ice from clearing. The boys and Angeline stayed close to the camp. Their impatience to reach Koonar's grave had been whetted by Elaitutna's story, and they found the waiting very hard. Nevertheless, there was nothing to be done about it. Awasin employed himself overhauling the party's gear. Jamie spent much time with Ohoto — who had taken a particular fancy to the white youth — trying to learn something of the Eskimo language. Angeline and Peetyuk seemed to be together a good deal — a fact which Jamie did not overlook.

The period of foul weather came to an end, and a week

after the visit to Elaitutna, Peetyuk announced that the river was sufficiently free of ice to permit canoe travel. It was decided that they should start for Koonar's grave the following morning, using their own two Chipeweyan canoes and accompanied by Ohoto and Kakut in kayaks. The dogs were to be left at the Eskimo camp under the care of Bellikari.

The Stone House — as they continued to think of the grave mound — was about thirty miles downstream on Innuit Ku from the camps. The current ran so fast that it took the party only half a day to reach the rapids where Jamie and Awasin had wrecked their canoe the previous summer.

The cataract was not yet in sight, although its roaring voice filled their ears, when Kakut led the flotilla to the shore. The kayaks and canoes were hauled up on the bank and the party went forward on foot.

As they looked down over the foaming white torrent, Jamie and Awasin exchanged glances. Peetyuk noticed the exchange, and shouted out so that everyone else could hear, "You two angry we not run rapids? Eskimo big coward? Only white man and Cree got brave enough run big rapid like that."

"Cut it out, Peetyuk," Jamie answered. "We weren't brave. We were darn fools, and you know it!"

"You only shy," Peetyuk said, grinning. "When we go down Big River to coast maybe you show poor Eskimo boy how run big rapids too. I learn quick from you I bet."

The exchange was cut short by a gesture from Ohoto, who had reached the crest of a low ridge ahead of the rest.

He was pointing to the north, and as the others climbed up beside him they stopped and stood in silence looking out over a thaw-flooded valley toward a rocky hill upon whose crest stood a massive stone structure.

This was the Stone House they had come so far to seek. This was the grave of Koonar, the Man of Iron.

CHAPTER 14

Koonar's Grave

On that spring day the unending sweep of rolling plain held a quality of desolation which even the hard white sunlight could not dispel. The land seemed unutterably empty, devoid even of the memory of living things. No birds sang. No caribou moved across the monochromatic wilderness of rocky ridges, sodden tundra, and melting drifts. The mosses and lichens underfoot were not yet quickening. They remained duncolored in their winter lifelessness.

This was the Barrenlands at its most somber hour, freed from the winter sleep but not yet stirring into the short summer frenzy of new life. It was a gray-faced corpse.

Angeline, Awasin and Jamie all felt the oppressive sense of lifelessness and involuntarily moved closer to one another. The Eskimos and Peetyuk were not immune to it either. Ohoto muttered something almost under his breath, and Kakut nodded his heavy head.

"They say they stay here. Wait for us," Peetyuk told his friends. "Not go Koonar grave. I not feel happy go there either; but if you go, I go."

Jamie shook himself and tried to speak briskly.

"Let's not start acting like a bunch of kids in a haunted house. There's nothing to be scared of. Awasin and I spent a night alongside the Stone House and I crawled right into it. I know it seems pretty spooky, but there's no such thing as ghosts anyway. Come on, lets go."

Awasin and Peetyuk glanced at each other and Awasin answered for both of them.

"Perhaps there are no spirits in your own country, Jamie. Perhaps white men have eyes that do not see what we see. White men know many things but they do not know *all* things." He shrugged and turned to pick up his carrying bag. Slinging it over his shoulder, he turned back to Jamie. "Even the blind hare feels the presence of the great white owl," he concluded, and strode off toward the distant loom of the Stone House.

The other three fell in behind him and Jamie had nothing to say. Not for the first time, he was dismayed by the reactions of his companions. "Some day I'll learn to keep my big mouth shut," he muttered ruefully as he trotted to catch up to Awasin.

They crossed the broad swampy valley, sometimes wading knee deep in the icy thaw water, and then began to climb the rock-strewn slope of the ridge where the tomb stood. The Stone House took on stature as they came closer, so that it seemed to dominate the land. This was an illusion, for the structure was not more than fifteen feet square and ten feet high. Yet the illusion had reality to it, for in a land which was otherwise devoid of any indication that men had ever passed this way, this single creation of human hands became the focal point in a sea of emptiness.

As they climbed over the sharp-edged, frost-shattered boulders below it, the visitors felt an oppressive sense of dislocation. Again they seemed to have stepped out of the realm of familiar things into an alien and infinitely older world.

Awasin stopped when he was ten feet from the tomb. Paying no attention to the others, he rummaged in his carrying bag and took out a plug of tobacco. He laid it down on a flat rock.

Peetyuk stepped up beside the Indian. Taking a skin-wrapped package of dried deer meat from his own bag, he laid it down beside the tobacco.

Jamie watched this performance with a puzzled frown on his face but held his peace. His restraint was rewarded. Awasin had been sharply observing his white companion, and when Jamie made no flippant comment and showed no sign of impatience, he explained, a little shyly, a little awkwardly.

"We think it is a good thing to make gifts to those who have gone, Jamie. We have much, for we are alive. They have nothing, for they are dead. When you and I were here last year I forgot what is due the dead. But I told myself that if I came back I would not forget again." His voice became almost pleading. "Perhaps you think we are foolish, but do not laugh about it. I ask you not to laugh."

Jamie shook his head. "I never felt less like laughing," he replied solemnly. He dug in his pocket and pulled out a highly valued pocketknife which he had won as a school prize in Toronto years ago. He glanced at Awasin in some embarrassment. "Can I? Is it all right if I give something too?"

Peetyuk caught Jamie by the left arm, and squeezed hard. "That *good* you do that, Jamie."

There was a warmth in his voice which Jamie had seldom heard since their fight at Kasmere Lake. He stepped forward and laid the knife on the rock. Angeline followed him and placed a packet of tea beside the other gifts.

There was a new buoyancy in Awasin's voice, as though he were relieved of some deep inner tension. "I am sorry for what I said about your people, back at camp. There was a shadow coming between you and us, and it was partly my fault. There is so much anger in our hearts against white people that sometimes we turn upon our friends. You *are* our friend; Angeline's, mine and Peetyuk's. We were wrong to turn our faces from you."

"I never turned mine," Angeline interjected tartly. "Speak for yourself, brother. You forgot that I *like* porcupines."

"And that means *I'm* a porcupine?" Jamie asked. "Okay, Angeline, you're right. I am. And since everyone seems to be being sorry around here, I might as well tell you *I'm* sorry for the way I acted too. Now let's get on with what we came to do."

Massive and forbidding, Koonar's tomb had been built with great care and labor in the form of what appeared to be a solid cube of rocks whose interstices had been close-packed with muskeg sods. These sods had taken root and spread, giving the whole structure a mossy overlay. However, the appearance of a solid cube was an illusion, as Jamie had discovered the previous year. He had found a small, half collapsed tunnel leading under the north wall into an inner crypt, and had crawled inside. Now he led the way to the tunnel entrance. He stopped abruptly as he saw a white, domed object lying on the moss nearby. Peetyuk saw it at the same time and gasped.

"Don't get jumpy, Peetyuk," Jamie said hastily. "It's only a skull. It was inside the cache and I pulled it out without knowing what it was when I crawled in there last summer. We'll put it back where it belongs."

Peetyuk was not reassured. He backed quickly away from the tomb and Awasin, who had seen the skull the previous year and had been badly frightened at the time, stepped back with him.

"I not go in!" Peetyuk said shakily. "I sorry, Jamie. I not go in!"

"There's no need," Jamie replied. "I'll do it. Awasin, help me roll away the stones."

Reluctantly Awasin came forward and the two boys removed the stones with which they had blocked the narrow entrance after their previous visit.

The tunnel was no more than a crevice in the rocks, floored with thick moss and illuminated only by faint gleams of light filtering through the interstices in the boulders. Jamie bent down to peer into the opening and he could just distinguish the outlines of the things he had briefly removed and then hurriedly thrust back into the tunnel before he and Awasin departed overland to the westward. His own heart was beating faster than usual, and he felt a strong revulsion at once again having to enter that wet, dark hole.

He took a deep breath before working his head and shoulders into the entrance. His hands touched chill metal and he wiggled quickly out again, dragging the object with him.

Peetyuk and Angeline gazed in amazement at an immense weapon, nearly four feet long and heavily encrusted with rust and dirt.

"Koonar's knife!" Peetyuk muttered in a shaken voice.

"It's a sword, Peetyuk," Jamie explained. "A two-handed sword. Only a giant of a man could have handled a thing like this. I can hardly heft it at all. Here, Awasin, lay it down easy on the moss. There's an awful lot of rust. Probably not too much solid iron left in it."

Having taken the first plunge, Jamie turned back to the entrance with less reluctance. He brought out a rusted iron helmet next, and after that a dagger whose blade had been reduced by rust to a flaking filament of metal.

"That's all I took out last year," Jamie explained to Peetyuk and Angeline. "Now I have to crawl right inside and see what's left. I'm going to light matches so I can look around."

"You will only find bones, Jamie," Angeline said timidly. "Perhaps you should not go inside. Perhaps we should be satisfied with what we have."

Jamie shook his head stubbornly.

"No," he said. "I have to see what's there. And I have to put the skull back where I found it."

Awasin joined Jamie at the entrance and squatted down uneasily as Jamie began wriggling into the tunnel. Peetyuk and Angeline stood a few paces away. Peetyuk's eyes kept shifting from the entrance to the white skull that seemed to stare blankly at the sky out of empty sockets.

Jamie had disappeared from view. There was a scratching sound as he lit a match, then his muffled voice could be heard.

"I'm inside, Awasin. It's like a cave. About three feet high. You'll have to pass the skull in to me."

Overcoming his revulsion, Awasin forced himself to pick up the skull. He carried it very gingerly to the entrance and thrust it into the darkness where Jamie took it from him.

For an unbearably long time there was no further sound from the tomb. Then Jamie's muted voice was heard again. It sounded strained.

"I'm passing out some more stuff. You'll have to stick your head in, Awasin. Be careful. It's something like a box, but it's as heavy as a rock."

Steeling himself, Awasin knelt down and thrust his head and arms into the musty-smelling hole. His hands came into contact with a cold, slimy surface and he shrank back involuntarily. Then a match flared and he saw Jamie's face, white and streaked with sweat and altogether fearful-looking. Awasin almost scrambled out of the entrance.

"Get hold of it," Jamie said impatiently. "It's only a box. It won't bite."

As the match flame died Awasin looked down and saw that the object was a greenish square thing with a lip all round the top. He forced himself to grasp it and squirmed back out of the hole. Jamie was right behind him.

Jamie got to his feet and stood for a minute breathing deeply.

"That's enough of *that!*" he said when he had got his breath. "Let's have a look at the box."

On closer examination the "box" turned out to be a sort of casket carved out of soapstone, about ten inches square and eight inches deep. At one time it must have had a wooden cover, but this had rotted away, leaving only fragments of wood clinging to the thick rim. The box appeared to be filled with black mold, but when Jamie cautiously lifted some of this material with a stick he encountered hard objects underneath.

The boys and Angeline crowded close around the stone box, their uneasiness forgotten. Gingerly Jamie lifted one of the objects out and cleaned the decayed vegetation off it with his fingers. It was revealed as an open circlet, like a bracelet with a piece missing. It was of some very heavy metal and was dull greenish in color. Jamie scratched the surface with his thumbnail.

"I think this might be gold!" he said in hushed tones.

Fired by the treasure fever, Peetyuk grabbed a stick and began poking in the debris. But Jamie caught his arm and stopped him.

"Hold on, Pete. We'd better not muck around with this stuff any more. Might smash up something in there that's gone rotten. We'd better leave the box just like it is until some expert can go to work on it."

"It not box," Peetyuk replied. "That only old kind Eskimo cook-pot, made of stone."

"Whatever it is, it seems to be full of Koonar's things," Angeline interjected. "I think Jamie is right. We should wrap it up in moss and put it in one of the carrying bags."

Jamie waved his hand at the sword and dagger lying on the turf nearby.

"We're going to have trouble with those, too. Looks to me like they're so rusty they'd break into a hundred pieces if they got one good bang."

"I fix," said Peetyuk, anxious to redeem himself after Jamie's rebuke. "We take sticks and put along sides. Then wrap tight in wet deerskin. Skin dry and shrink. Make hard cover, very strong, not bend."

Awasin nodded. "That will do it. But first we must get these things back to the Eskimo camps. Each of us can carry one thing, and if we are careful, nothing will be broken."

They did not linger at the tomb. But before they departed Awasin collected the small pile of gifts from the flat rock and placed them in the entrance tunnel. Then he and Jamie rolled several big boulders over the opening.

Half an hour later they rejoined the two Eskimos on the far ridge. Kakut and Ohoto glanced at the things the young people were carrying, but made no comment. Get-

ting lithely to their feet, the Eskimos led the way back to
the kayaks and canoes.

Late that night, when the camp had gone to bed and the
four were alone in their tent, Peetyuk volunteered some
information.

"I not tell before, but last week some people talk, talk
about you take stuff from Koonar grave. Some people go
Elaitutna tent and he make drum dance and call spirits.
People hear strange voice, very deep, speak words nobody
know. But hear three times name 'Koonar.' Elaitutna listen
with eyes shut. He shake all over. Then Elaitutna fall on
floor like dead man. After a while he wake up and say is
very bad take things from Koonar grave. He say make
Koonar very angry, give us bad luck."

As Jamie listened to this recital he had a hard time trying to suppress the skepticism he felt. Nevertheless he
held his peace until Peetyuk stepped outside the tent for a
moment. Jamie turned to speak to Awasin then, and he
was startled by the expression of uneasiness on the Cree
youth's face.

"What's the matter with you?" Jamie snapped. "*You*
don't swallow all that stuff, do you?"

Awasin looked unhappy. "I do not know what to think.
We too have medicine men, Jamie, and they can do things
you would not believe. I do not know if Koonar's ghost
spoke to the people, but I do not like this talk about bad
luck. The Eskimos may not want to help us now, and if
they do not we cannot hope to find the canoe route eastward to the coast. That would be very bad luck for us, I
think."

Peetyuk's return forced Jamie to swallow the sharp retort which sprang to his lips. He contented himself with a mild comment.

"Uncle Angus says everyone makes his own luck and I believe him. We'll make out all right so long as we don't get scared by a lot of mumbo-jumbo. Now let's forget it and turn in. There's plenty of work to do tomorrow."

CHAPTER 15
Interlude

Eᴀʀʟʏ ᴛʜᴇ ɴᴇxᴛ ᴍᴏʀɴɪɴɢ ᴛʜᴇ boys and Angeline began preparing the Viking relics for the long trip to Churchill. Peetyuk got the frame of an old kayak from one of his Eskimo friends, and from it they took several long stringers with which to splint the sword.

They were busy fitting these splints when the tent flap was pushed open and old Elaitutna shuffled in. It was the first time he had visited them and they did not quite know how to receive him. However, he ignored their awkward attempts at a welcome and, going straight to the sword, squatted down beside it.

Delicately he touched the heavy haft where several greenish metal rings hung loosely around the remains of what had once been an ivory or bone handle. Then he barked a command at Peetyuk, who hastily brought out the dagger, the helmet and the stone pot.

The old man gave the dagger and helmet only a perfunctory glance, but he looked at the stone casket with such concentrated attention that the youngsters began to feel uneasy. Jamie moved forward, intending to pick out the metal armlet to show to the *angeokok*, but the old man stopped him with a fierce gesture.

Then Elaitutna fumbled in a skin pouch which hung from a lanyard over his shoulder and clawed out a small packet of dried skin. It was so black and filthy that the youngsters could make nothing of it. The old man thrust it toward the casket and mumbled a few phrases before stuffing the black thing back into the pouch. Then he got to his feet, uttered a harsh burst of words, pushed open the tent flap and vanished without a backward glance.

"Now what the heck was all *that* about?" Jamie asked.

Peetyuk's reply was subdued and hesitant. "He very angry man. That thing he take from pouch is very strong charm. When he hold it up he say to pot: 'Bring no evil to me. Not my fault someone dig up your bones. Fault belong Kablunait and Itkilit — white men and Indians.' Then, when he go out of tent he say we are big fools and all Eskimo who help us they bigger fools."

Peetyuk was badly upset by the visit, and Awasin too was much disturbed. Jamie tried to dispel the effect of the visit.

"Look, you fellows. We're not going to let that old geezer scare us, are we? Maybe he talks to ghosts, and maybe he doesn't. But we're not doing anything wrong. Archaeologists dig up graves every day all over the world, and nothing happens to them. Nothing's going to happen to us, either."

"I not know what people do other places," Peetyuk stubbornly replied. "But I think it bad thing wake up dead men in *my* country. Elaitutna, he say it very bad."

Although he was exasperated by Peetyuk's attitude, Jamie had learned not to show his impatience. He was trying to find some way to ease his friend's fears without antagonizing him, when Angeline unexpectedly came to his rescue.

"What Jamie says is true, Peetyuk. We are doing nothing bad to Koonar. It will help the Eskimos and I think Koonar would have wanted that. And I do not think everyone agrees with Elaitutna that we are doing a bad thing."

Jamie snatched gratefully at this support, even though it came from a source of which he did not entirely approve.

"Elaitutna's only one man. Let's go talk to Ohoto. He's the best hunter in the camp and everyone looks up to him. We'll explain exactly what we intend to do, and maybe he'll take our side."

To the youngsters' great relief Ohoto agreed that the removal of the weapons from the grave was no great crime, particularly since the sale of these things to the white men in the south might enable the Eskimos to obtain guns and ammunition. But Ohoto had reservations about the stone casket. He told the young people that according to Elaitutna it reputedly contained the arrow that had killed Koonar and — grisly thought — some of the blood Koonar had shed through his death wound.

Peetyuk shuddered visibly as he translated this, and even Jamie felt a twinge of unease. He mastered it firmly.

"I just don't swallow that," he said. "How can Elaitutna be sure what's in the casket? Maybe the arrowhead is there, but all that stuff about blood is more than likely something he invented to scare us. I think he wants that casket for himself. Whatever he has in mind, we're going to take it with us. I'll carry it myself and I'll look after it. None of the rest of you even need to touch it. Tell Ohoto that, Pete. Ask him if he'll still help us."

There was a moment's silence after Peetyuk had translated this. Ohoto looked hard and long at Jamie before replying slowly.

"He say," said Peetyuk, "maybe you foolish, but you brave too. He say he help us. He show us way to Big River when time to go."

"What about you, Pete? Do you feel okay about it now?"

"Maybe I foolish too, Jamie. But I just as brave as you. We take stone pot!"

During the next ten days the weather rapidly improved. Summer had already begun in the Barrens, where there is no real spring as we know it. Winter ends with a roar of thawing rivers, and almost before they are clear of ice the country is inundated by a wave of living things who have no time to waste if they are to raise their young before the return of the frost.

Gulls, wading birds, ducks, geese, and small land birds seemed to appear almost instantaneously and in such numbers that the sound of their myriad voices made an unending chorus that never ceased, even in the middle of the night. But then, there was no longer any real darkness at night, for the sun barely sank below the horizon and its glow never left the sky.

The herds of doe caribou had long since disappeared, hurrying north to the fawning grounds. Most of the herds of bucks had followed them at a more leisurely pace, but there were still many loitering bucks scattered across the plains.

On sandy ridges exposed by the melting snows arctic foxes, dun-colored after the loss of their white winter coats, barked and yapped outside their burrows. At the mouths of larger dens on higher ridges, small brown wolf puppies scuffled with one another and crawled over the bodies of their patient parents.

Everywhere the muskegs were alive with mouselike lemmings. On stretches of drier ground, golden ground squirrels sat up like posts and whistled at each other and at the rough-legged hawks that spiraled overhead.

The dead land was dead no longer. The Barrens were vibrant with the brief burst of summer life.

During this period the boys and Angeline were busy making ready for the journey to the coast. Despite an increasing display of animosity from Elaitutna, the majority of the Eskimos remained well disposed to the young travelers and were ready to lend them a hand with their preparations. The older hunters pooled their memories of the Hudson Bay country in order to help Ohoto decide upon the route to be followed. Kakut and Bellikari agreed to collect the cache which the boys had left on Little River, and to keep the boys' dogs for them through the summer. Kakut, Ohoto and two other men would journey south to Thanout Lake that coming winter as soon as ice and snow made sledding possible. They would bring the dogs with them, as well as the surplus possessions which the youngsters would be unable to carry with them to Hudson Bay. On their return journey to the Barrens it was hoped that the Eskimos would have a good load of rifles, ammunition, tea and flour purchased with some of the proceeds from the sale of the Viking relics.

Angeline took on the task of repairing the clothes and soft gear. She had so much help from the Eskimo women and girls that she found she was hardly allowed to do anything herself. However, the women encouraged her to learn how to make waterproof Eskimoan skin boots. Peetyuk's mother was particularly attentive to Angeline, and whenever Peetyuk appeared she addressed remarks to him which made him blush and sidle off. Neither Angeline nor the boys could understand what the Eskimo woman was saying and Peetyuk refused to translate, but it was not too hard to guess the gist of the remarks.

"Looks like Pete's mother's made her choice of a daughter-in-law," Jamie announced innocently to Awasin one morning. Peetyuk, who was sitting nearby oiling his rifle, pretended not to hear, but it was impossible to ignore Awasin's reply.

"You are right, Jamie. And do you see how my sister is sewing clothes in Eskimo style? I hope Peetyuk will be a good husband. If he starves her, I will have to beat him, for a brother must look to his sister's welfare."

This was too much for Peetyuk. Jumping to his feet, he sprang roaring at his two friends, but they were ready for him. Catching his arms, they wrestled him to the ground. Jamie sat on him while Awasin, with great solicitude, felt Peetyuk's forehead.

"He is hot, Jamie. Love fever, I think." He raised his voice and shouted. "Angeline! Come quick. Peetyuk is sick. He is calling for you!"

Angeline had been sewing in one of the Eskimo tents. Now she flew to the travel tent. One look at the tableau on the ground showed her she had been tricked. She said not a word but grabbed the water pail, and before any of the boys could blink an eye she had doused all three of them with a stream of icy water. Whereupon she turned and tramped off to the Eskimo tent without a backward glance.

Spitting and gasping, the boys struggled to their feet.

"Anyway," said Awasin when he had got his breath, "Peetyuk is cool again . . . for a little while!"

As June drew to an end the atmosphere in the Eskimo camp began to undergo a subtle change. Although most of the Eskimos remained friendly and helpful, they began to show symptoms of uneasiness when they were in the presence of the three boys. Awasin was quick to notice this, and one evening he queried Peetyuk about it. At first Peetyuk was evasive, but finally he admitted that there was trouble brewing.

"Is Elaitutna. He say bad things going to happen to us, and if we stay Eskimo camp bad things happen to Eskimos too. He tell people we never get to Hudson Bay. He say Koonar not let us carry his things to strange land. He tell Ohoto he never come back alive if he go with us."

"The old devil's just jealous," Jamie burst out angrily. "He's run things here for a long time, and look at the mess the Ihalmiut are in. Just because it looks like we can help them when he can't, he's out to stop us."

"I think we should talk to Ohoto again," Angeline said quietly but firmly. "You are angry, Jamie, and that will not help anyone."

Several Eskimos were with Ohoto when the youngsters entered his tent, but these people quickly found excuses to get up and leave. Ohoto himself seemed subdued and uncomfortable. However, when Peetyuk explained why they had come, he showed relief.

"I am glad you know what is happening," he explained through Peetyuk. "I did not want to tell you myself, and that made me unhappy, for there should be no secrets between friends. Now I will tell you the rest. Elaitutna had another spirit-talk and most of the People were there. At the end of it Elaitutna said Koonar had cursed you and had warned all the People to have nothing more to do with you. Now the People do not know what to do. Some even say I should not go with you; but I am not a sick old man who is afraid of spirits. I *will* go with you as far as Big River. And I think it would be well for us to leave as soon as we can, for the People are listening more and more to Elaitutna. They are growing afraid, and frightened people can do strange things."

"How soon can we go, then?" Jamie asked anxiously.

Ohoto wrinkled his heavy brows. "We cannot go until a strong wind comes to break up the rotten ice in the big lakes. I hope it will come soon. I do not trust Elaitutna, and if anything should happen to your canoes in the meantime you would never be able to make the trip."

"He wouldn't dare do anything!" cried Jamie, but there was no conviction in his voice.

Later that night when they were back in their own tent, the youngsters found it hard to go to sleep. They discussed the situation until well past midnight without finding any solution. Finally Angeline went outside to light a fire and boil the kettle for a mug-up of tea. When she came back her eyes were gleaming with excitement.

"Listen," she said. "The north wind is coming. Already you can hear it, and the sky is growing dark with clouds. Perhaps it will blow hard enough tonight to break the ice."

By the time they had drunk their tea the wind was rustling through the camp, and its hopeful sound finally lulled them to sleep. When they woke at dawn they found a full gale blowing. As they scrambled out of their tent they met Ohoto coming to waken them. He greeted them with a smile.

"Eat quick," he told them, "for there is much to do. The ice will go today, and tomorrow we will go too."

CHAPTER 16

Lake-in-Lake

All day while the strong wind blew the travelers worked to complete their preparations. Awasin inspected the canoes very carefully, checking every seam to make sure the spruce-gum seal was still sound. The others spent their time assembling the gear and supplies.

They had decided that they should travel as light as possible. Everything which could be dispensed with was to be left behind. Spare food was given away to the Eskimos, and Awasin and Peetyuk left behind their rifles, together with most of the ammunition, for the Eskimos to use. They calculated that one rifle and fifty rounds would be sufficient for the journey to the coast.

The balance of the luggage included sleeping robes, the tent, two travel bags containing spare clothing, skeleton cooking gear, two hatchets, a coil of rope, tea, salt, flour, dried deer meat — and the Viking relics. These last had been carefully splinted and wrapped in two deer-hide parcels and were tied one to a canoe, beneath the thwarts so that in the event of an upset they would not be lost. It was arranged that Jamie and Peetyuk were to paddle one canoe while Awasin and his sister would paddle the other.

Shortly after dawn the next morning the voyagers prepared to embark. Not many Eskimos showed up to see
them off. Only Peetyuk's friends and relations were on
hand, and there was none of the good-natured badinage
and horseplay which usually marks such an occasion. People moved about quietly and solemnly, helping the boys
and Angeline load the canoes. Peetyuk's mother had just
brought down a farewell gift of boiled meat when there
came a hoarse shout from the high bank overlooking the
river beach.

Everyone turned to look, and there stood Elaitutna, a
black and forbidding figure against the dawn sky. For
some minutes he remained motionless. Then he raised a
short deer spear in his right hand and shook it fiercely in
the direction of the voyagers, at the same time shouting
harsh words in his old, cracked voice.

There was a murmur of fear from the assembled Eskimos and for a moment it looked as if they would turn and
run. But Ohoto jumped forward, raised his fist at the old
angeokok and yelled a challenge in return. Elaitutna lingered only a moment longer, then vanished.

Ohoto's face was grim as he turned to where Angeline
and the boys stood uncertainly by the canoes. He spoke
sharply, and Peetyuk translated in a shaky voice.

"Elaitutna has cursed us himself, but I have told him
that if any harm comes to you four, I will put a knife under his skinny ribs. Come now, it is time to go."

The youngsters needed no urging. Peetyuk disengaged
himself from his mother, who stood motionless with tears

running down her cheeks. Kakut and some of the other men carefully slid the canoes into the water and the travelers jumped aboard. In a moment they were out in the stream following Ohoto, whose slim kayak shot ahead.

Angeline turned for a last glance at the silent people standing against the backdrop of squat, skin-covered tents and rolling gray plains stretching to the horizon behind them. Despite herself she could not repress a shudder at the thought of Elaitutna, whose malice seemed to follow them as they began this voyage into the unknown country to the eastward.

A mile northeast of the camps Ohoto led the canoes into the mouth of the small river where the deer-spearing had taken place. There was a swift current in this stream and the paddlers had to strain to make progress, but after some hours of hard work they entered a small lake which they coasted to its southern end.

Here they found an even smaller stream which was so shallow that they had to get out and walk alongside the canoes. The boys were grateful for the thigh-length skin boots, called *kamikpak*, which the Eskimos had shown Angeline how to make. These were of parchmentlike deer hide, minutely stitched with a thread made of deer sinew. Before being worn the boots were filled with water, allowed to stand for a few minutes, and then emptied out. The water swelled the sinew thread, thus making the seams watertight and at the same time softening the hide so that the boots became supple.

Ohoto did not have to tow his kayak. When the water became too shoal he simply hoisted it up and carried it balanced on his head while he walked merrily along, shouting back for the rest to hurry up.

The stream ended in a pond which was soon crossed, and this was followed by a long portage across a low, gravel ridge to the foot of Wolf Lake. By the time everybody and everything was across the portage it was mid-afternoon and Ohoto suggested that they camp.

"Eskimo not hurry when start trip," Peetyuk explained to his friends. "Start slow. Go quicker later. White men start fast, slow down later."

Jamie did not rise to the bait. The truth was that twenty miles of hard upstream paddling and towing had made him quite ready to accept Ohoto's suggestion. He only grinned at Peetyuk and replied. "Me Eskimo now. Me go slow, you bet!"

They camped that night less than eight miles as the crow flies from the Innuit Ku camps, having made a semi-circular detour in order to follow the water routes. But canoe travel in the north seldom follows a direct line and one grows used to paddling thirty or forty miles in order to make ten in any desired direction.

They made better progress the next day. Ahead of them, stretching out of sight to the southeast, lay the twenty-mile length of Wolf Lake. Only two days previously its waters had been imprisoned under five feet of ice. This ice had been rotted by the spring suns and when the gale struck the lake it turned to mush and disappeared. As the canoes and kayak set out down the western shore the following morning, the boys could see no trace of ice at all.

There was little wind that day and the lake stayed smooth. All morning they coasted its flat, barren shores southward.

A good-sized river ran out of the lake towards the southeast. It was swollen with flood waters and carried the canoes and kayak along at a good three knots. The little flotilla fairly flew downstream. There were no rapids to cause trouble, for this river ran through level country.

"This is the stuff!" Jamie cried to Peetyuk in the bow. "A week at this rate and we'll be at the coast!"

"Ho! A week? Maybe a month! You wait. Not go so easy in little while."

"It can't be too tough, Pete. I've been on plenty of bad

rivers down in the forest country. Big River can't be any worse."

"No bad rivers in south!" Peetyuk said disdainfully. "Baby riding in moccasin go down *those* river okay. Not like Big River. Ohoto say only big fish, and strong fish too, get down *that* river."

Half an hour later Ohoto, who had gone on far ahead and had landed on an island in a lakelike expansion of the river, signaled the canoes to put in to shore. He had a fire lit and the tea billy on the boil. Peetyuk carried the grub-box up to the fire where Angeline made bannocks.

As they munched their bannocks and drank their scalding tea, the boys questioned Ohoto about the country they were going through. Peetyuk translated Ohoto's reply.

"Now we are on Koonok — No River. He get this name because he got so many lakes, but no rapids. He is half river and half lake. He runs to Lake-in-Lake. This big lake, sits on island, and there is even bigger lake around it.

"It is secret place. Very hard find way in. In old, old times Itkilit come out into plains looking for Innuit one summer. They know Innuit living on Koonok, and so they come in four bands, many canoes and many men. One band comes from east, one from west, one from south, one from north.

"But man called Yaha hunting deer see Itkilit coming and run to Innuit camp with news. Nearly one hundred Innuit in that camp, but maybe three hundred Itkilit coming. Innuit not know what to do. Women all wailing and children crying. Then man named Kahutsuak gather all and speak: 'Take all kayaks. Make women sit on decks and tie children on behind. Nighttime leave camp with all fires going, all tents standing, dogs tied near tents. I take where we safe.'

"Everyone do what Kahutsuak say, and he lead kayaks by secret way to Lake-in-Lake and to island in middle of inside lake, and Itkilit never see. Then Kahutsuak say: 'All must sleep in holes in ground. Raise no tents. No person make fire. In daytime, no person walk around against sky.'

"Itkilit bands meet on Koonok and find Eskimo camp. Attack it, but find nobody there — only dogs and empty tents. Itkilit very angry. Spread out and search everywhere for sign of where Innuit go, but not find any sign.

"At island in Lake-in-Lake Innuit have very hard time. Cannot cook food, heat water, get warm. Rainy days come and people soaking wet. One woman there, Pameo, very pretty woman, very strong in mind. She say to herself: 'Itkilit never find this place, why should I freeze to death?'

"One night she slip away from camp and hide behind sand ridge on island. In morning she light little fire and cook some fish. It very little fire, but make some smoke. That morning Itkilit men standing on only hill where can see Lake-in-Lake. Itkilit men see smoke.

"Next morning terrible yell from all around island and Itkilit canoes land all around. Great battle then, but Itkilit men too many, and after fighting done not one Innuit still alive except Pameo, who off by herself and Itkilit never see.

"Pameo come back when Itkilit gone, and find all dead.

Then she tear clothes and hair and cry a long time. Afterward she never leave that place. Old men say she still there, still crying in nighttime. Sometimes, old men say, little smoke come from island. But no Innuit go there. That island called Place of Bones."

After lunch they continued southeast down the stream. Toward evening the Koonok gave up all pretense of being a river and spread out into a maze of island-studded channels. Ohoto turned and twisted through this maze until he led the canoes out onto a larger body of water surrounded by low, barren muskeg plains. Only one small, mounded hill broke the bleak monotony of the landscape and Ohoto headed his kayak toward it and made a landing near its base.

This was weird country. The low and featureless terrain, coupled with the formless and complicated outline of the lake, made it impossible to get any clear idea of what the place was like. Islands could not be distinguished from points, nor points from the main shore. Everything seemed to blend into one hazy, shapeless world with a nightmare quality of unreality.

"I think I am lost already," Awasin commented as he and Angeline landed their canoe and joined the others on the shore.

"*All* Indian get twisted here," Peetyuk replied. "Never mind. We climb little hill, then maybe you see straight."

Leaving Ohoto to start a supper fire, the four youngsters trudged up the gentle slope, wading almost knee deep in saturated muskeg. When they reached the low crest they turned about.

In the last glittering rays of the fading sun Lake-in-Lake lay revealed to them. Its waters extended from the northward like two gigantic arms, embracing an almost perfect circlet of land which appeared to be fifteen or twenty miles in diameter. This circlet of land in turn enclosed another big lake in whose center lay a large island; and from the center of this island gleamed the water of yet another lake.

"That where Innuit hide from Indians," Peetyuk explained as he pointed to the island, "and this is hill where Itkilit see Pameo's smoke."

Jamie shivered as he looked out over the flat, monochrome expanse of drowned lands, tundra and lakes where not a tree or a rocky ridge rose to break the monotony.

"Come on," he said, "before *we* start seeing smoke out there!" And he led the way back to the tiny campfire which glowed dimly against the darkening waters of the lake below.

It was not much of a supper. Camp that night was on a tiny strip of gravel beach barely raised above the lake level. There was no other place to pitch the tent, since the whole country hereabouts was one vast drowned bog. There was only damp moss to burn, and it took Ohoto an hour to boil the kettle. There was no point in trying to cook anything, so the travelers contented themselves with a meal of cold bannock and hot tea before crawling into their robes. They slept badly, and all night long Peetyuk muttered and whimpered uneasily as if his dreams were haunted by the spirit of desolation which plagued this place.

CHAPTER 17

Anoeeuk

THE NEXT MORNING DAWNED GRAY
and somber. While a breakfast fire was being lit a fine gray
drizzle had begun to fall and it was difficult to boil the kettle. The travelers were in a gloomy state of mind as they
climbed into their canoes and set off across the open
water through the drizzle.

"You made enough noise last night to wake the dead,"
Jamie remarked to Peetyuk some time after they had
started. "What was the matter with you, anyhow?"

"That bad joke, Jamie," Peetyuk replied soberly, resting
his paddle for a moment. "No talk of waking dead. Last
night I think I hear Elaitutna talking. He say we *stay* in
Lake-in-Lake. Leave our bones with Innuit who die here
long ago."

Jamie, his nerves strained by the brooding atmosphere
of the place, lost his temper.

"Oh, for heaven's sake, Pete, lay off that stuff. What on
earth can stop us from getting out of here?"

"*That* can stop us, Jamie." Peetyuk pointed toward the
east where a gray, wavering wall of fog had appeared over
the horizon and was advancing toward them.

Ohoto had also seen the approaching wall of fog and now his kayak shot between the two canoes while he shouted a warning. "He say hurry, hurry," Peetyuk translated. "*Hikikak* come. Rain-fog make us blind, then *anoeeuk*, big wind, catch us. We not know where shore is. Big waves maybe sink canoes."

There was no mistaking the urgency in Ohoto's voice. The two canoes followed him with all the speed the paddlers could muster as he drove his kayak toward the nearest piece of land — a low, rocky islet in the middle of the lake. Canoes and kayak seemed to fly over the leaden surface of the water, but fast as they went *hikikak* moved still faster. They were still half a mile from safety when the world vanished. It was as if they had paddled into a black and dripping tunnel. Awasin and Jamie, in the stern of their respective canoes, could barely see Angeline and Peetyuk in the bows. It was only by shouting that the canoes and kayak could keep touch with one another at all.

The gray rain-fog was so thick as to be almost solid, but as yet there was no wind. The muffled reverberation of Ohoto's voice guiding the two canoes was the only sound in the sinister silence.

Really frightened, the four youngsters paddled with the strength of desperation. No one wasted breath trying to talk, but each of them secretly wondered how Ohoto could possibly manage to find the little islet now. Their hearts were pounding with effort and with apprehension when first Angeline and then Peetyuk yelled a warning as the two canoes surged over a ledge of rock that lay barely below the surface.

Ohoto emerged out of the darkness and grasped first one canoe and then the other, lifting the bows up on the shore of the islet. The youngsters sprang ashore and at his snapped command picked up the canoes and carried them bodily to the center of the islet. Ohoto's kayak was already there, and now he instructed them to fill the canoes with loose boulders, while he did the same with his kayak.

Staggering about in the dripping darkness, the youngsters tripped and bumped into each other, and fell helplessly over unseen obstacles.

"What's going on?" Jamie yelled plaintively as he strained to lift a heavy rock into the canoe. "Has Ohoto gone nuts? What are we doing this for?"

"Not talk, just work," Peetyuk grunted in reply. "You see pretty quick what happen. You not make bad joke about dead men again, I bet."

The travelers were still ballasting the canoes when the wind struck. This was *anoeeuk*, a fearsome gale which is called a line squall on the open ocean, but which also blows over the great plains of the Barrenlands. *Anoeeuk* strikes out of a dead calm and wind velocities mount instantly up to as much as a hundred miles an hour. It gives no warning except for the sullen darkness of the sky which precedes its coming. It does not last long, but while it blows there is not much that can resist its power.

When *anoeeuk* struck Lake-in-Lake it spun Jamie right around. He felt a hand grasp him and fling him to the ground, then someone fell on top of him. It was Ohoto, whose other arm was tight around Angeline's waist. Peetyuk had meanwhile grabbed Awasin and the two boys rolled into the lee of the canoes.

It was impossible to stand up. The wind was like a solid battering-ram and the canoes began to shift and grind ominously on the rocky ground. Ohoto thrust Angeline into Jamie's arms, and on hands and knees scrabbled to the nearest canoe, where he flung himself over the gunwale to help hold it down. The grinding stopped but now a new threat appeared.

The shallow waters of the lake had been whipped into foam and short, high waves were marching angrily against the islet. With every minute they grew in size. Spray from them was soon whipping right across the islet, and it was obvious that in a few more minutes the spray would be followed by solid water.

The hurricane had blown away the fog, but it was still impossible to see much, due to the spray. Jamie caught a glimpse of Awasin and Peetyuk, who had joined Ohoto and were clinging to the gunwales of the second canoe. "Can you stick it out alone?" he bellowed in Angeline's ear.

Angeline was wet and cold and miserably uncomfortable, and she was also frightened. But she did not intend to let Jamie see any signs of weakness in her. Bravely she shouted back at him: "I am all right. You go."

Slipping free of her, Jamie crawled toward the others. Ohoto gestured toward the kayak, which was jerking like a wounded bird trying to fly. Jamie changed course. Reaching the fragile Eskimo boat, he crawled over it so that it lay under him. As he did so a gigantic wave broke just short of the kayak, drenching him with solid water.

Numbly the five people clung to the rapidly flooding islet. There was nothing more they could do. Each of them was aware of the cold finger of death reaching out to touch them . . . and there was nothing they could do.

Then, as suddenly as it had begun, *anoeeuk* ceased to blow. The sky began to lighten. The roar of the hurricane vanished, to be replaced by the thunder of surf upon the islet.

Shaken and white-faced, the four youngsters got to their feet and stood beside Ohoto. They looked out over the lake and saw that its entire surface was a contorted mass of breaking waves in which no canoe could have lived for more than a few moments. On the windward side of the islet the waves were reaching fifty feet in from the shoreline, almost to the center of the rocky little sanctuary.

Although the rain-fog was gone, the sky was still overcast and the scene was dreary and desolate beyond belief. Ohoto's face was gaunt with strain — and perhaps with something else — as he muttered a few words to Peetyuk.

"He say we safe now," Peetyuk interpreted. "But only his *tapek* — his good luck — make it so. Very strong *tapek*. Too strong for Elaitutna."

Jamie glanced at his friend, but the derisive remark with which he once might have replied to such a statement was never born. Jamie had nothing to say.

It was well into the afternoon before the seas died down enough to make it safe to continue the voyage. When the canoes and kayak were again launched on Lake-in-Lake, the occupants took to their paddles with something close to frenzy. No one slacked off until Ohoto led them into a little cove on the southern mainland shore. A little stream ran from the south into the bottom of this cove.

"Now we leave dead land," Ohoto told them with un-mistakable relief.

CHAPTER 18

The Deer's Way

STILL SWOLLEN BY THE SPRING floods, the stream offered hard going at first and there were many places where the boys and Angeline had to get out and track the canoes through shallow rapids. But after a time they reached a little lakelet upon whose southern shore they saw a dwarfed clump of willows. They headed for this meager "bush" with as much joy as if it had been a full-fledged forest.

Cheering them even more, the skies began to clear. In short order they had a roaring fire going and were soon cooking a huge meal of meat with which to still the rumblings in their empty stomachs.

"Good country now," Peetyuk said. "See? Many deer paths on the shore."

During the rest of the day, as they worked their way south over small lakes and ponds to the portage over the height of land, the country came more and more alive. Mating ducks disported themselves on every pond. Twice they saw smoky brown arctic foxes watching them from sandy ridges. Flock after flock of shore birds skittered along the fringes of the lakes. Towards evening when they had crossed the short portage and were descending another small stream, they saw above them a herd of buck caribou standing on a gravel ridge. Although still in velvet, and only partly grown, the deers' antlers loomed against the sky like a spreading forest.

Ohoto looked keenly at the herd and then shouted something to Peetyuk, who grinned and translated for the others.

"Ohoto say we come good time. He say tomorrow reach greatest deer path in world. Maybe we see *tuktu-mie*, the Great Herd."

Although enough daylight was left to travel by (at this season there is no real night on the arctic tundra since the sun barely sets before it rises again), Ohoto called a halt and camp was pitched on the ridge where the bucks had been. No effort was made to shoot one of the deer, for there was still fresh meat in the canoes and neither Eskimos nor Indians kill game unnecessarily.

With a comfortable little fire to warm and cheer them, the boys sat sipping tea after their evening meal. Angeline was busily stitching up rents in their *kamikpak* where these had been torn by sharp stones during the wading in the streams.

"What is the Great Herd, Peetyuk?" Angeline asked.

"Is like this, Angeline. *Tuktu* — the deer — they never still. In spring they move long way north, like the birds. When winter start, they move long way south, like the birds. But in summer they move too. About July all deer from all over gather in big herds, then suddenly start south. One big mob of deer. But when they get to edge

of forest, big mob breaks up, and all start back north again. When they go south in July, that when we see the Great Herd. Deer come over country like swarm of flies then. Flatten out whole country where they go! Most famous place for Great Herd we call Deer's Way — at north end Nuelthin-tua."

"I have heard my father speak of such a herd," Awasin said. "Our people have never seen it, but the Chipeweyans used to tell of it. I thought it was all finished now, that the deer were not plenty enough to make great herds."

"Maybe finish soon," Peetyuk replied. "Not finish yet. Maybe see tomorrow. *Tuktu-mie* . . . deer come like flies. . . ."

He was interrupted by a resounding whack as Jamie slapped the back of his own neck with his open palm.

"Speaking of flies, I'm being et alive! Where in heck did all the mosquitoes come from? There's still snow in the gullies, but here they are!"

There was no doubt about it. An all-pervading hum was rising in the night air, and out of nowhere clouds of viciously hungry mosquitoes swept down upon the little camp. These were the first of the Barrenland mosquitoes. Tough, tiny, insatiable, they appear while snow is still on the ground and stay until late summer. On calm days they make life miserable for all warm-blooded beasts. Fortunately there are few calm days on the great plains, or life there would be unendurable in summertime.

Unhappily for the travelers it was calm this night, and as the hum rose to a roar they were driven to take refuge in their sleeping bags with their heads well down under

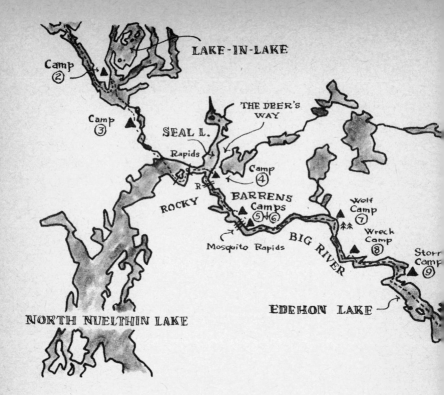

the robes. The choice was to suffocate or be eaten alive, and suffocation seemed preferable.

Dawn brought a westerly breeze and relief from the plague of mosquitoes. The voyagers breakfasted and all morning they worked down the little stream. Shortly before midday they reached the shores of the northeastern arm of Nuelthin-tua.

Since leaving the northwestern bay of this mighty lake several weeks earlier they had made a great circle. With the difference in the seasons, the nature of the lake had completely changed. Far to the south there were still patches of ice, but for the most part the lake was open,

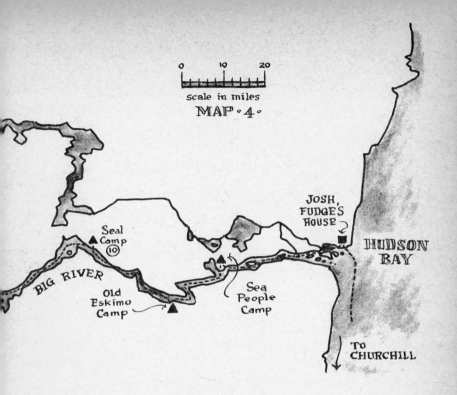

whipped with white wind-lop as the canoes ventured out
upon it.

Fortunately the arm they were in was filled with a mass
of islands which provided shelter for the canoes; otherwise they would have had to camp until the wind blew
itself out.

Led by the agile Ohoto in his slim little kayak, the flotilla dodged from lee of island to lee of island for several
hours. In the early afternoon they reached a bay from
which a short, savage stretch of river drained Nuelthin-
tua. The outlet gorge had been carved deep into the gray
bedrock and the roar of its rapids could be heard for a
long time before the voyagers reached its lip.

They went ashore at the head of the short, steep run, and the boys and Angeline were very quiet as they looked down the foaming cataract. Ohoto glanced at their thoughtful faces and grinned. Making them a low bow and giving a comic skip, he jumped into his kayak and shot straight out into the foaming maelstrom.

Angeline muffled a little shriek and the boys gasped. The kayak slipped over the lip of a six-foot backwave, poised for a second on the crest like a bird about to take flight, and then shot out of sight into a curtain of white water. It reappeared seconds later, going like an arrow, with Ohoto wielding his paddle so furiously that it made a blur of reflected light over his head. Seconds later the kayak leaped out of the lower cataract and came to rest, perkily swinging around on a quiet backwater eddy, while Ohoto waved an arm at his companions and beckoned them to hurry up and follow.

Jamie was incredulous. "I never thought that crazy little boat would last one second!" he said.

"Crazy boat? Ho!" Peetyuk replied indignantly. "Crazy like a fish! Eskimo kayak he go anywhere. Now we see if Indian canoe, he half as good!"

With some reluctance the four took their places. Jamie took the responsible stern position in one canoe and Awasin in the other. Despite taunting gestures from Ohoto, they approached the lip of the rapid with excessive caution, back-paddling hard until the current finally gripped them and they had no choice but to drive on down.

Once the first instant of doubt was over, they all began to experience the wild exhilaration of running white-water rapids and drove their canoes forward, adroitly steering them from side to side of the run in order to miss the bigger waves. They shot out at the bottom seconds later, unharmed although half soaked with spray.

Ohoto greeted them with a shout of laughter, then spun his little craft around and went skittering out onto the open waters of the new lake which stretched ahead.

"Eskimo call this Netchilikuak — Seal Lake," said Peetyuk in reply to a question from Jamie. "Supposed to be seals swim all way up here from ocean. Maybe true — maybe not."

"It's good news if it *is* true," Jamie replied. "If a seal can get *up* Big River, we can surely get *down* it."

"You run one rapid, now you talk big," Peetyuk cautioned him. "Paddle more hard, talk more less or Ohoto lose us."

The canoes and kayaks made a fast crossing of the six-mile width of Seal Lake, for the wind was now behind them. Well before twilight they brought up on a long, jutting sandspit along whose base a frieze of willows promised fuel for a campfire.

The land beyond their camp was a narrow isthmus some five miles long running north and south and separating Seal Lake from another, larger lake to the eastward. Low and level, this isthmus formed a natural highway for the migrating herds moving north or south up the hundred-mile-long eastern shores of Nuelthin-tua. This was the first point at which the herds could pass the barrier of the great lake. The Eskimos knew it as the Deer's Way, and it was evident to the visitors that deer in countless thousands must have used the way recently.

Even while they were pitching camp the travelers could smell a strong barnyard odor. When they walked up on the flat muskeg beyond the beach they discovered that it had been churned into an immense chocolate-colored pudding by the feet of innumerable caribou.

As they watched, they saw a slow-flowing wave of darkness, like molasses, pouring down a distant hill at the northern end of the isthmus. As it came closer it resolved itself into a herd of over a thousand bucks, marching fifty or sixty abreast, moving with such an irresistible motion that Jamie felt a touch of panic.

"We better get out of the way," he yelled to Awasin and Angeline, who stood a little distance from him.

"Be brave, Jamie!" Peetyuk called back. "Deer not eat you. You stand still, you see what happen."

Much as he wanted to retreat to the shore, Jamie could not do so as long as Peetyuk stood his ground. However, Awasin had Angeline to worry about and, preferring caution to bravado, he led his sister to the edge of the isthmus as the great herd approached at a long, space-eating lope.

When the head of the throng was no more than two hundred yards from the three small figures standing in its path, the lead bucks caught the human scent. Some of them flung up their heads, snorted loudly and tried to halt. But the pressure of the multitudes behind them was irresistible and, jostled from the rear, they were driven forward.

Inexorably the mass of animals bore down on Jamie.

Wild-eyed, he spun around to see what Ohoto and Pee-tyuk were doing. To his amazement he saw that Ohoto was sitting down, filling his stubby little soapstone pipe, while Peetyuk was leaning casually on his rifle, whistling through his teeth.

Firmly resisting the impulse to take to his heels, Jamie cocked his rifle and held it in front of him. Then the deer were on him.

It seemed certain that he must be trampled underfoot; but at the last minute the mass of animals split away on both sides of him, passing no closer than ten feet.

The rumbling of the animals' guts and the musical clinking of their ankle joints filled his ears, while his nostrils were full of the sweet, rank smell of the beasts. His fear began to evaporate, to be replaced by a strange excitement and by a feeling of awe such as he had never known before. So much tumultuous life swirling past him, unhurried and unafraid, stirred him to his inner being. A feeling of affinity, almost of love, for these magnificent, imperturbable animals swelled through him. When the herd had passed by he remained standing as if entranced, staring after them until they were far away.

Peetyuk joined him, and the Eskimo boy's face was sober.

"You feel it, Jamie? The Spirit of the Deer. Now you know how Eskimo feel about *tuktu*. *Tuktu* give Eskimo his life. *Tuktu*, he is our brother."

CHAPTER 19

The Curse of Flies

T<small>HE BIG HERD WAS FOLLOWED BY</small> several smaller herds and Ohoto shot a particularly fat buck from one of these. Angeline went back to camp with a piece of back meat to cook for supper while the boys and Ohoto quartered the beast.

That night they stayed up late, talking by the fire. The next morning they would reach Big River, where Ohoto was to leave them.

Their knowledge of what lay ahead of them was very scanty. All they really knew was that the river would eventually take them to Hudson Bay; that there were several lakes along it; that it was almost one continuous rapid and ran with a tremendous current; and that they might hope to meet sea Eskimos near the coast. Consequently, the boys were not at all anxious to say good-by to Ohoto. Jamie was tempted to ask the Eskimo if he would go with them as far as the coast, but his pride would not let him. In any case, he knew that Ohoto would have found it almost impossible to fight his way back up the river. A trip on Big River was one-way — downstream only.

Next morning the campers were reluctant to wake up. It

was a gloomy, slow breakfast. Ohoto finally broke the spell. With a good-natured shout he tousled Angeline's hair, pushed Peetyuk flat on his face in the sand, and trotted off toward his kayak, his small bundle-bag on his back.

This little bit of horseplay roused the boys and they soon had the tent down and their gear in the canoes. Then, under a blue sky and with a light riffle of wind to help them along, they set out for the head of Big River.

They had barely entered Big River Bay, a couple of miles from their overnight camp, when Angeline held up her paddle.

"Listen," she asked. "What is that?"

The boys strained to hear a low, muted muttering like the sound of distant summer thunder.

"Rapids, or a falls," Awasin said in a small voice.

"*Big* rapids!" Peetyuk added. "We still many miles from end of bay. Very big, or we not hear upwind."

Ohoto, who was well ahead, beckoned impatiently with his paddle and the boys and Angeline again took up the stroke. But they were very subdued and not a word passed between them as they paddled on. The thunder grew in volume as they neared the end of the bay.

They beached their canoes on a point of land at the river mouth and, led by Ohoto, climbed a low ridge to see what lay ahead.

What they saw was enough to shake the confidence of the bravest of canoemen. They seemed to be standing on the raised edge of an immense bowl. To the eastward the land sloped away to a dim and distant horizon, and down this endless slope plunged one of the biggest rivers in the Barrenlands.

It did not flow between well-defined banks like an ordinary river. It spilled over the edge of the bowl and roared down the rocky slope in one mighty cataract of foam and spray that seemed to stretch for miles.

The river was formidable enough, but the land through which it ran was even more fearsome to behold. It was a totally dead land, so strewn with frost-shattered rocks that it looked like one titanic slag heap. Nothing, not even a caribou, could have crossed it on foot. Only the roaring river offered a passage to the east.

Ohoto stared glumly at the river for a long time. When he turned toward the boys again his usually jovial face was creased with lines of worry. He spoke to Peetyuk in a low voice.

"Ohoto say he never see Big River before except in wintertime when all frozen up," Peetyuk translated. "He say he never know she such bad river. He say maybe better go back to Innuit camps and take canoes south by way we came, or wait till winter and take dogsleds south."

Peetyuk and Awasin looked at Jamie.

"No, we can't do that," Jamie said slowly. "Remember Elaitutna and the way the Eskimos were acting when we left? If we went back that old devil would say we had to, because of the curse, and then he'd have all the people on his side. They'd probably never let us get clear with the Viking stuff. Anyway, if we *did* go south the way we came the chances are we'd be picked up by the police even before we got to The Pas. And we'd never get past The Pas without being caught. Either we have to go down Big River or admit we're licked and lose the Viking stuff. One thing though, I think it's too big a risk to take Angeline with us any farther. Anything could happen to us on this river. I think she ought to go back with Ohoto and come south to Thanout Lake with him in the wintertime."

Jamie had meant well by this suggestion, but the girl's reaction was as furious as if he had struck her in the face. With blazing eyes she faced him, so tense with anger that Jamie backed up a step.

"You will *not* leave me behind!" she cried. "Many times you have tried to do that, Jamie. I think you hate me because I am a girl. But I am as good a traveler as you are. Perhaps I am better. After all you are only . . . only a white man!" She almost spat out the last words.

Roughly Awasin caught her arm and pulled her back.

"Be quiet, sister!" he said sharply. "Jamie does not hate you. He is afraid for you. And you will not have to go back to the Eskimo camps. You are almost a woman now and you may make your own choice. But act like a woman!"

It was Peetyuk who smoothed out the quarrel.

"We look after Angeline easy. We not able let her go back anyhow. Who would paddle with Awasin, eh? One fellow alone in canoe not live long on *this* river."

"Look, Angeline," Jamie said placatingly, "I wasn't trying to be mean. I was just scared something might happen to you. But you're pretty near as good a 'man' as any one of us, and Peetyuk's right, we need you. No hard feelings?"

Angeline's burst of temper had been short-lived. Shyly now she touched Jamie's arm.

"I am sorry, Jamie. And you will see, I will be no trouble. Now I think we have talked long enough. Men always talk too much. Let us go before there is another argument."

"Right," Jamie said. "If we stand here looking at this mess of white water much longer we'll get too scared to lift a paddle."

The leave-taking from Ohoto was brief and unemotional. Since they had made up their minds to go on, he accepted the decision without comment. He rubbed noses with Angeline, whacked each of the boys heartily on the shoulder and, singing a snatch of Eskimo song, trotted to his kayak, pushed off, and was soon winging up the bay with never a backward look. Eskimos believe it is bad luck to look back at a leave-taking.

The voyagers lingered a little longer on the ridge, assessing the river and the rapids and making a plan for running the first part of it. Now that they were committed, their lethargy seemed to vanish.

"It is best we start down the center channel," Awasin suggested. "Once we are past that little island we can swing to the south channel. Beyond that we will have to see. I will lead for the first part if you wish. Then we can take turns picking the channels."

"Good enough," said Jamie. "Okay, you crowd of *voyageurs*, let's see what we can do with this Big River!"

As the canoes swung out into the oily funnel which marked the head of the first chute, all four paddlers were tense and strained, their mouths dry, and their eyes staring. But as they entered the slick water and were swept swiftly into the first rapids the high excitement of the moment gripped them. In the lead canoe Angeline swung her paddle expertly, reacting instantly to Awasin's commands. And that normally staid youth was soon shouting and whooping like a movie Indian while his little canoe shot back and forth from eddy to eddy like a scared trout. Jamie and Peetyuk were close behind, Peetyuk's red hair flying in the wind of their passing, and Jamie's eyes as bright as a squirrel's as he searched the foam for signs of rocks ahead.

Once started there was no stopping. For what seemed like hours, but was in reality only fifteen or twenty minutes, the headlong plunge continued. Then, at a sharp bend in the river, the two canoes whipped out into a small lake and the paddlers had time to catch their breath.

"Wheee-ew!" Jamie shouted. "That's better than a roller-coaster! This old river's not so bad! We never so much as ticked a rock. How about you, Awasin?"

Awasin grinned and wiped his brow. "I have a good bow paddler. She is a better woman than I am, anyway."

"I should *hope* so," Jamie laughed. "Well, come on, sports, let's not hold back. At this rate we'll be in Churchill tomorrow night!"

For the next several hours the run continued. Alternating with long stretches of white water were several small lakes, but even in these the current flowed at two or three miles an hour. By mid-afternoon the constant excitement and tension had begun to tell on the youngsters, and when

Awasin detected a deeper note in the roar ahead he swung to shore, and the others followed, glad of a chance to rest.

It was as well they went ashore when they did.

When they clambered up on the bank to stretch strained muscles they saw ahead of them a cataract which made the rapids they had already run look like riffles in a gutter.

Up to this point Big River had been playing with them. Now it showed its teeth. As far downstream as they could see there was no water — only a mass of foam punctured by the sleek wet shapes of innumerable boulders. The river seemed to have spilled right out of its bed and to be running hog-wild over a land that sloped steeply down to the eastward.

The exhilaration of the past few hours vanished.

"*That's* not a rapid!" Jamie muttered. "I don't know what to call it, but I know one thing . . . no canoe can go down there."

No one argued with him. For a long time they stared in apprehensive silence, broken finally by Peetyuk.

"Now I think maybe Ohoto right. Maybe should go back and try some other road."

"We cannot go back," Awasin replied. "We have been running more than five hours now. You forget the speed of this river. To go back we would have to track the canoes upstream for thirty or forty miles. We would be many days, and it is much more dangerous to track up on such a river than to run down it."

"Awasin's right, we can't go back," said Jamie. "We have to go on . . . but how?"

"Only one way," said Peetyuk. "Make big portage. This country all flat. Not like country we just come through. Got no hills, no rocks, easy to walk. We got not much to carry. Canoe, they light. We do easy, eh?"

"It's walk or stay, I guess," Jamie answered. "But let's camp here tonight. I've had enough of Big River for one day!"

The next day was one which none of the four would ever forget. Dawn brought gray skies but not a breath of wind. Long before daylight the mosquitoes arrived. And with them came the second of the Barrenland plagues — black flies.

Black flies breed in the eddies of swift water, and Big River mothered them in myriads. The flies swarmed over the youngsters in such numbers that a haze formed around their heads. Flies crawled into every crevice in their clothing, and when they found flesh they bit, leaving a little drop of blood and a rising welt that itched furiously.

Once out of their sleeping bags the travelers found it impossible to remain still long enough even to light a fire and get some breakfast.

"Come on! Come on!" Jamie yelped. "Grab the stuff! We got to get out of here!"

Wordlessly, Awasin seized one canoe and Peetyuk grabbed the other. Flipping them upside down they hoisted them to their shoulders and set off at a dog-trot over the saturated muskeg. Jamie and Angeline followed close behind, festooned with packs, robes and paddles. Not everything could be carried at one time and so some of the bundles were left for a second trip.

They fled, but they were hotly pursued. The cloud of insects kept increasing in size. Awasin and Peetyuk had to use both hands to hold the gunwales of the canoes steady, and so could not beat off the swarms which crawled over their faces, into their eyes, up their nostrils and into their panting mouths. They had not trotted more than half a mile when they were forced to fling down the canoes so they could flail away at their tormentors.

Jamie and Angeline were not much better off. When they caught up to the other two, they also flung down their loads and joined in the mad dance.

"I can't stand this!" Jamie cried. "We got to do something!"

"Open the packs! Get out the spare shirts," Awasin commanded. "Wrap them around your heads and over your faces. Tie up the wrists of your jackets. It will help a little. We must go on. Maybe we can find a clump of willows by the river and build a smudge."

"Leave canoes here," Peetyuk added in a muffled voice as he wrapped a long flannel shirt around his head. "We run quick. Find wood, make big smoke!"

Thrusting the bundles under the canoes, the others followed his advice and soon the four of them were running over the sodden plains as if beset by devils.

Half crying with fatigue and misery, they stumbled into a little valley through which a tiny stream ran down to Big River and in this protected place they found a copse of

willows. Tugging and pulling at the green branches like wild animals, they soon piled up a high heap. With trembling hands Awasin touched a match to some dry moss which he stuffed under it.

The wood was green and wet and burned slowly and with no heat — but it was not heat the travelers wanted. Great coils of yellow smoke rose from the smoldering mass and hung low in the still air. One after another the four flung themselves into the smoke, only to be driven out again coughing and spitting and with their eyes streaming. Each time they emerged they were met by a new wave of flies and driven back again.

The hours that followed were sheer agony. The choice was one of being choked to death or of being driven mad by the flies. When deliverance finally came in the form of a heavy rain followed by a rising easterly wind, all four were at the end of their endurance.

The relief of being free of the flies was so great that they ignored their soaking clothes and the chill of the east wind and lay in exhaustion on the saturated moss until Awasin roused them.

"We must go back to the canoes. If this wind gets too strong it will turn them over and all our gear will get wet."

"Let it rain! Let it rain!" Jamie cried. "Boy! I never thought I'd live to bless the rain. Okay, Awasin, you're right as usual. Let's go."

They plodded back across the dark plain to the abandoned canoes. There was no point in trying to move on until the rain let up, so they crawled under the canoes, and there, wet and shivering, they put in the rest of that miserable day. Towards night the rain slackened to a drizzle and they emerged, stiff, swollen and utterly dispirited, to lug the canoes and gear to the little valley. After a long struggle they finally got another fire to burn but it could not be made to boil the tea pail, and so they had to content themselves with a mug of warm water each, instead of tea. Wearily they erected the tent and crawled into it.

Lying all together in one wet huddle, like half-drowned pups, they finally dozed off, but not before Peetyuk had spent several moments mumbling mysteriously in Eskimo.

"What are you up to, Pete?" Jamie asked him.

"Not laugh at me, Jamie. I make old medicine song to Spirit of the Wind. I ask him blow and blow and never stop blow."

"*Laugh* at you? Listen, Pete. You tell me the words and *I'll* sing too. I'd rather have a hurricane than face those flies again!"

Whether the Wind Spirit heeded Peetyuk's song, or whether luck was simply with the travelers, the wind kept blowing all that night and shifted to the north. The morning dawned clear and cool and free of flies.

After a hearty breakfast the travelers again took up their loads, and led by Peetyuk, who seemed able to find firm footing in the worst of the muskeg, they continued their portage.

It was not as long a march as they had feared. Some five miles from the head of the wild cataract they came to the borders of a good-sized lake. Here Angeline and Awasin set up camp while the other two went back to pick up the balance of the gear. It was almost dark before they returned, but a big fire and a huge meal of meat roasted on long sticks over the coals was waiting for them.

They snuggled into their robes tired but content. Ahead of them lay several miles of easy paddling on quiet waters. They did not let themselves think about what might lie beyond the lake. The two Crees and the Eskimo boy had known from early childhood that one must live each day without worrying overmuch about what the following day would bring. Jamie was learning that this was an essential attitude for those who had to live the nomad life. He was phlegmatic as he sleepily summed up the trip that night.

"It's sure a crazy country. One day we whip along like an express train and go maybe forty miles. The next we crawl like a sick lemming. Ah well, some day we'll get there . . . I suppose."

CHAPTER 20

Of Wolves and Sails

On the following day, their third on Big River, the travelers made good progress. A light wind kept the flies at bay and helped the canoes along. Not that they needed any help, for Big River continued to flow downhill at an appalling speed. The voyagers had only to paddle hard enough to keep steerageway on the canoes while the current carried them along sometimes at eight or nine miles an hour.

Rapids were frequent, but the boys and Angeline were becoming hardened to them. During this day they ran twelve major rapids and innumerable smaller ones without mishap.

Being more relaxed now, they had more time to look about them, but there was not much to see. Big River continued to carry them through flat tundra country. Towards evening, the monotony of the barren plains was broken by a range of low hills. Everyone kept a sharp lookout for spruce thickets. The Eskimos had told them they would touch the edge of timberline just before reaching the only really large lake on Big River.

As they crossed a little lake in early evening Peetyuk, in

the bow of the lead canoe, gave a shout and pointed with his paddle. Under the southern slope of a high sand esker they all could see a tiny stand of woods. Excitedly they headed for it and beached the canoes on a fine sand beach a few feet from the "forest."

It was a pathetic forest, consisting of a few dwarf black spruces that looked more like bushes than trees. These were the tough outriders of the forests to the south. Here on the edge of the open plains they somehow managed to survive. When Jamie chopped one of them down he discovered from the rings in the wood that it was over a hundred years old even though it was no more than six feet tall.

For the first time in weeks the travelers were able to have a really big, hot fire that night. They luxuriated in the joy of leaping flames, while their bedding and clothing hung steaming on surrounding trees.

The heavy dusk which passed for darkness in the summer Barrens had settled over the land, and Peetyuk and Angeline had already crawled into their sleeping bags. Jamie and Awasin were having a last mug of tea when Jamie stiffened, spilled half his tea, and hissed at Awasin.

"Look! Down by the beach!"

Awasin turned his head, and what he saw made the hairs on his neck rise. Not more than thirty feet away sat two immense white wolves with eyes glowing green in reflected firelight.

For a moment both boys were too startled to move.

Then Jamie cautiously reached out his hand for the rifle. Never taking his eyes off the wolves, he dragged the gun slowly toward him, worked the lever to shove a shell into the breech, and began to raise the muzzle.

"Wait, Jamie!" Awasin whispered. "Don't shoot. They mean us no harm. See? They are just curious."

Somewhat dubiously Jamie lowered the rifle. But as the shock of the encounter began to wear off he realized that Awasin was right. The wolves made no hostile moves but continued to stare with open curiosity at the two boys.

Finally the smaller of the two wolves — the female — got to her feet, shook herself like a dog, and with several slow, tentative wags of her bushy tail advanced a few careful steps toward the fire. She looked very much like an enormous and friendly husky, and the last of Jamie's panic vanished.

"I think they do not see men before," Awasin whispered. "They do not know enough to be afraid of us. Watch now; I will throw them the bones from supper."

Rising slowly to his feet, Awasin stepped away from the fire and picked up several rib bones. At his first movement the nearest wolf froze in her tracks, with one leg lifted, while the larger wolf got to his feet and backed off a little way.

Awasin began to make a low rumbling growl, like that of a dog who wishes to make friends with another dog. At the sound the ears of both wolves pricked sharply forward.

Carefully Awasin tossed the bones toward the wolves and then rejoined Jamie by the fire.

"They don't know what to make of us," Jamie muttered. He could hardly refrain from chuckling, for the wolves looked thoroughly puzzled and kept glancing at one another as if to say, "What should we do next?" Finally the female timidly edged forward until she could snatch one of the bones, whereupon she turned and fled down the beach as if all the devils of hell were after her. Her mate followed close on her heels.

Awasin laughed outright.

"They will have a tale to tell their pups. Their den must be close by — perhaps in the esker. That is a favorite place for wolves to make their homes. Maybe in the morning we will have time to look."

In the morning Jamie told Peetyuk and Angeline about the visitors, and Peetyuk grew most excited.

"*Amow*, the wolf, he my spirit-friend. All Eskimos have some kind animal for spirit-friend. Maybe wolf come visit me and I asleep. They think I poor kind of friend. I go look for house and tell I sorry." And with that he scrambled to his feet and went loping up the steep side of the esker.

Half an hour later, when the rest of the party had broken camp and was ready to leave, Peetyuk reappeared. He was grinning broadly and in his arms was a gray bundle of fur that squirmed to be put down.

It was a wolf pup, and when Peetyuk put it on the ground the roly-poly beast scampered off on its short legs to sniff at Awasin's feet. It was not the slightest bit afraid.

"You say hello to little *amow*," Peetyuk told his companions. "He not stay long. Must go back to house. See? Old wolf watch." He pointed to the crest of the esker where both adult wolves stood, nervously twitching their tails.

"My gosh! You're taking an awful risk, Pete," Jamie exclaimed. "Even a dog will go for you if you touch her young."

"No fear, Jamie. Wolf and me all friends. They know we not hurt. Often Eskimo boy play with wolf pup at their houses."

"He is so nice I would like to keep him," Angeline said, getting down on her knees to fondle the pup's ears.

"He more better stay in own country," Peetyuk told her gently. "I take back now. You wait, I not gone long."

Picking up the pup, which promptly began to chew at one of his ears, Peetyuk turned and began to climb the ridge. To Jamie's amazement and alarm the wolves did not back away but waited until Peetyuk passed not more than two yards from them. Then they trotted close behind the Eskimo.

"I wouldn't have believed that if I hadn't seen it," Jamie said in awe-struck tones. "If Pete can charm wolves like that, he could charm any kind of wild animal there is."

Awasin grinned. "That is true, but I think he charms wild Cree girls best of all."

Everyone was in a good mood as they all set off that morning. Jamie even risked making a small joke on the subject of curses, which had been a taboo topic between him and Peetyuk. As the canoes rounded a point after running a short rapid, he remarked amiably:

"Looks like our luck has changed, Pete. Unless you

count the flies, we seem to have got out of range of old Elaitutna's bad medicine."

But this was a subject that Peetyuk was still not prepared to take lightly.

"We not come to Churchill yet," he said shortly. "Better you keep eyes open and mouth shut."

A sharp lookout was certainly essential on Big River, which was becoming more and more like a slalom slope. Rapid succeeded rapid all day long and it was seldom that the youngsters could relax for more than a few moments at a time. But they were becoming increasingly skillful and they were making such good time that instead of camping

early they continued to run downstream until almost dusk. Jamie and Peetyuk were in the lead as they swung around a sharp bend and entered a steep, roaring chute at a point where the river narrowed. The rapid was a bad one, and the travelers would normally have halted to reconnoiter before attempting to run it, but they were full of confidence and Jamie elected to head straight into it.

He and Peetyuk had their hands full, for there was a ledge right across the river halfway down where a huge curling backwave reared up as a solid wall of water. Their canoe shot through this wall without mishap, although both boys were drenched. There was a deep pool below it,

and here the two boys held the canoe in check while they waited for Awasin and Angeline, whose canoe was not far behind.

But as he approached the wall of white water, Awasin suddenly changed course, attempting to swerve to the left where the wall looked a little less fearsome. Before Angeline could grasp what her brother's intentions were, the canoe had swung sideways. An instant later it was out of control and was flung up on the backwave broadside-to.

While Jamie and Peetyuk watched in helpless horror the canoe vanished in the boiling spume. Split seconds later it emerged below the ledge, but upside down and barely showing above the surface. To the watchers' inexpressible relief they saw that both Angeline and Awasin were clinging to the wreck.

It was only a matter of moments for Jamie and Peetyuk to reach the waterlogged canoe, grab it by the bow, and haul it to the shore of the eddy pool where Awasin and Angeline struggled ashore, gasping for breath and looking like drowned rats. Then all four grabbed the swamped canoe and hauled it high and dry.

Angeline and Awasin were nearly paralyzed with cold. Peetyuk rushed to get a fire going, using a supply of dry wood brought with them from the previous campsite. Meanwhile Jamie hastily unrolled his and Peetyuk's bedding so that the boy and girl were able to shed their soaking clothes and cover themselves with something dry and warm.

Then Jamie and Peetyuk turned to the task of rescuing

the contents of the swamped canoe. Sleeping robes and clothing were spread out to dry on paddles propped up beside the fire. The precious bundle of Viking relics was examined and it was with great relief the boys found it had proved watertight and had suffered no damage. The canoe itself had a ten-inch gash along one side, but this was something which could easily be repaired with a strip of birch bark and some melted resin. All in all it appeared that the youngsters had come off lightly from what might well have been a fatal accident.

Relief at their narrow escape made everyone a little light-headed. Awasin was even trying to make a joke about his foolishness in trying to alter course when Pee-tyuk interrupted him.

"I not see rifle anywhere," he said quietly.

There was a moment of stunned silence.

"It was in the bottom of the canoe," Awasin cried in a stricken tone of voice. "I untied it when I thought I saw some caribou on the riverbank ahead of us . . . and I forgot to lash it down again . . ."

Full realization of what the loss of the rifle might mean was slow in coming. It was Angeline who finally put it into words.

"Without the rifle we can get no more meat. And we have so little food with us that we *must* have meat!"

Peetyuk nodded his head gloomily.

"If we not able shoot deer, soon we starve. Only food left in grub-box for two, three day."

"Look," Jamie said desperately, "that pool below the

rapid can't be very deep. And the water's clear as glass. Come on, Pete! It's still light enough to see. Maybe we can spot the rifle and dredge it up somehow."

Quickly the two boys shoved off in the undamaged canoe and paddled to the center of the pool, directly below the backwave. Jamie leaned over, staring into the water and probing with his paddle.

"It's no good," he said at last. "I can't see bottom, and I can't reach it with the paddle. Pete! Tie the hatchet on the end of the mooring line and drop it overboard."

Peetyuk lowered the hatchet over the side and when it hit bottom he hauled back the line, measuring it in arm's lengths as he did so.

His face was bleak.

"It more than ten feet deep, Jamie. I think we never find rifle down there."

Gloomily they paddled back to shore and told the others what they had discovered. The situation seemed hopeless. Neither Awasin nor Peetyuk could swim well enough to risk themselves on the surface of the rapid current, let alone underneath it at a depth of ten feet. And although Jamie was a strong swimmer he was not able to dive, for he had suffered from mastoiditis as a child and pressure on his eardrums gave him agonizing pain. Things looked very black indeed until Angeline spoke.

"I will dive for the rifle," she said. "It was partly my fault we lost it. If I had been quicker when Awasin turned we would not have upset. I am a good swimmer and I can dive very deep."

For an instant hope flared in Jamie's heart, then it died again.

"No, it wouldn't work, Angeline. That water's far too cold. You could never stand it."

Angeline's eyes blazed. "Perhaps it is too cold for *you*. But it is not too cold for *me*. I am a *Cree!*"

"My sister swims and dives like an otter," Awasin interjected. "But you are right, Jamie, it is too cold and too swift."

Angeline rounded sharply on her brother.

"Would you rather we all starve then? I tell you I can do it. I *will* do it!" She turned to Peetyuk who had been standing silent, undecided what to say. "Peetyuk. You believe I can do it. Tell them I can do it!"

Full of admiration for her spirit, yet convinced that the others were right, poor Peetyuk could do nothing but mumble inarticulately. For a moment Angeline stared at him coldly, then with a rapidity which left the boys helpless to stop her she flung off the sleeping robe and raced for the riverbank. Awasin gave an angry shout and started after her but he was too late. For a moment the girl stood slim and poised on the high cutbank, then she dived cleanly into the river.

"She's gone crazy!" Jamie yelled. "Grab the canoe, Pete!"

Leaving Awasin standing impotently on the bank, Jamie and Peetyuk flung themselves into the canoe and paddled frantically toward the middle of the pool. They gained on the sleek black head of the girl as she swam strongly for the backwave, but as Peetyuk leaned over to grab her she dived like a seal.

When she broke surface a few seconds later she was right under the lip of the falls. Before the boys could reach her she took a great gulp of air and again disappeared.

Awasin was desperate. He had waded out thigh-deep into the current and only Jamie's angry shout prevented him from plunging in.

"Don't be a fool, Awasin. You'll drown too. I'm going in for her . . . Pete, steady the canoe . . ."

Jamie had slipped off his moccasin rubbers and his jacket when Peetyuk yelled:

"She's up. Help me, Jamie!"

Almost capsizing the canoe, Jamie jumped to the bow. Peetyuk had hold of the girl by one arm but was unable to haul her up. Jamie leaned over and slipped his hands under both her arms. Pulling together, the two boys eased her up and over the gunwale. As she tumbled into the canoe there was a heavy thump against the wooden ribs. Clutched tightly in the girl's right hand was the missing rifle.

Angeline was almost unconscious and they had to pry the rifle out of her hand, which was as cold as death. Minutes later they had carried her to the fire and covered her with sleeping robes, and Awasin was forcing hot tea between her blue lips. Uncontrollable paroxysms of shivering wracked her whole body. Nevertheless she managed to force a small smile. Her voice was no more than a whisper and the boys had to lean close to hear what she said.

"A Cree girl can do anything . . . you see?"

Dumbly Jamie nodded. But Peetyuk, his eyes glistening with something deeper than admiration, leaned down and clumsily took the girl's hand in his.

"I see very good," he muttered huskily. "And I think we never forget what Cree girl, she can do."

CHAPTER 21

The Sea People

THE JULY DAYS SLIPPED PAST AND the travelers made steady progress to the east. Big River seemed to have settled down a little and although there were as many rapids as ever, most were passable — if barely so. Occasionally a really bad stretch necessitated a portage. The weather remained reasonably good and the voyagers were storm-bound only once, when a torrential rain and gale winds kept them in their tent for two days. Eventually they reached Edehon Lake — a mighty lake running thirty miles to the southeast. Carefully they coasted its indented shores searching for the outlet, which turned out to be on a hidden bay to the *northwest*. The search for Big River's outlet had cost them another two days.

The emptiness of the country they were passing through had begun to have a depressing effect upon them. Since leaving the Deer's Way they had come across no trace of human beings. There were no old campsites, nor even cuttings in the few spruce thickets they encountered. It was as if mankind had always avoided Big River, and the voyagers began to have an uneasy feeling that they had stepped out of the inhabited world into some lost wilderness.

But if there were no humans on Big River, there was other life along its banks. Several times they saw wolves, and almost every night their travel camp was visited by arctic foxes who were so fearless they would come right up to the campfire. On one occasion Angeline even coaxed a fox to take a piece of meat out of her hand.

Life on the river itself was abundant too. There were many geese and ducks, and the river held stranger beasts as well. One day, shortly after leaving Edehon, the travelers ran a steep rapid and emerged into a tiny lake across whose center ran a gravel bar. Jamie noticed three immense, shiny black rocks on this bar and he was about to draw Peetyuk's attention to the peculiar appearance of the rocks when one of them suddenly humped itself to the water's edge and vanished with an enormous splash.

They were still staring goggle-eyed at the place where the moving "rock" had vanished when Jamie realized what it was that they had seen. With a shout he headed his canoe toward the reef.

The remaining two seals waited until the canoes were less than a hundred feet away before they too humped their way into the water. Meantime Peetyuk had grabbed the rifle but he waited too long and the seals disappeared before he could shoot.

Jamie was much amused by Peetyuk's expression of bewilderment.

"Seals aren't caribou, you dope! They don't swim on *top* of the water. Keep your eyes peeled now. They'll pop up somewhere for another look at us."

A few seconds later a bewhiskered, sleek, big-eyed head reappeared close by. Its appearance was so sudden that Peetyuk was caught off balance and came within an ace of pitching out of the canoe to join the seal. Before he could recover himself and level his rifle the seal was gone again.

Angeline could not contain herself and broke into a shout of laughter as a second seal, which had incautiously surfaced right beside Jamie's canoe, went down again with such a powerful flurry that the spray flew into Peetyuk's face and momentarily blinded him.

"Leave them be!" Jamie yelled, at the sight of the wildly waving rifle barrel. "You'll shoot one of us. No use killing them anyway. They'll sink and we won't get them. Sit down and let's just watch."

Rather reluctantly Peetyuk sat down and laid the gun aside. The canoes drifted idly in the current and in a few moments all three seals had their heads out. They swam closer and closer, and occasionally one of them would lose his nerve. With a loud, wet *whoof* he would duck under until curiosity got the better of him and up he would come for another look.

Tiring of the show at last, the travelers took up their paddles and moved on — and so did the seals. They escorted the canoes the length of the little lake and left them only at the head of the next rapids, which was a particularly bad one.

"I read about 'fresh-water' seals once," Jamie told his friends as they were preparing to portage this rapid. "They're really harbor seals but some of them get a taste for fresh water and go way inland up rivers and lakes and never come down again. Scientists don't know much about them, and not many white people have ever seen them in the north. I guess we're lucky."

"I glad I not shoot," Peetyuk said. "They got face like funny old man. And they good sign. If seal come here, we maybe not too far from salt water."

The next morning, the fifteenth day after leaving the Deer's Way, they came out into the long westerly arm of a lake. As they were paddling under the lee of the rocky shore, Peetyuk began to wave his paddle wildly. Having caught everyone's attention, he pointed to a low ridge just back from the shore where, in silent welcome, stood a cluster of three *inukok* — Eskimo stonemen.

"Not far now!" Peetyuk cried. "Sea People must make those. Ohoto tell me late summertime they come upriver and camp to meet *tuktu*. Spend winter in country, and go back to sea in spring. We watch hard for camps."

But it was not a camp which gave them their first contact with the Sea People. Later that day, as they were again entering the river, they saw a big white canoe upside down upon a sand ridge a few hundred yards back from the shore.

Beaching their own canoes, the youngsters climbed the ridge. There was no sign of a camp nearby and the canoe itself was very old. Most of its canvas had rotted away leaving the wooden planking to whiten in the sun and gales.

Peetyuk stared at it with a puzzled frown, but Awasin and Jamie began to examine it more closely.

"Something underneath, I think," Jamie said. "Let's turn it over."

Both boys bent down and got a grip on the gunwale. They had to strain to lift it for this was no little river canoe — it was a twenty-two-foot sea-going one. With a sudden jerk they managed to raise it and at that instant Peetyuk yelled at them.

"No! No! Do not turn! Leave alone!"

He was too late. The big canoe teetered on its under gunwale and then fell right side up with a crackling sound.

"Not touch!" Peetyuk cried. "I fool. Not guess before. That sea man's grave!"

There was no doubt that he was right. Under the canoe lay a shapeless bundle of rotted caribou hides. Foxes and lesser beasts had rummaged it thoroughly, and here and there could be seen the white bones of a human being. Next to the body was a wooden box without a lid in which could be seen stone pipes and other personal oddments. Alongside the body lay a badly rusted rifle, a long-handled fish spear, and two broken paddles.

"We put back quick!" Peetyuk said, and his voice was sharp with perturbation. "Eskimo in our country bury dead people on top of ground and put tools and weapons with him for next world. My people put rocks on top; but Sea People put canoe on top."

He hurried to the canoe and the other two boys joined him without a word, for they had been shocked by the discovery of what was under it. In a moment they had levered the heavy boat back on its edge and then they lowered it gently into its former position over the dead man and his belongings.

Somewhat shaken, the voyagers hurried on downriver. But they realized that the great canoe had been a good sign too. It was obvious that the river below this point could not be very difficult to navigate, since otherwise no one would have brought a sea-going canoe this far inland.

Big River had indeed changed its nature. It was no longer flinging itself down a steady slope at express-train speed. Now it flowed more sedately through a dead-flat, drowned land of muskegs, bogs and innumerable ponds. Although the travelers did not know it, they were already on the flat coastal plain which borders Hudson Bay.

When they camped that night it was on a site that had been used by other people for many centuries. Here they found scores of tent-circles of round stones marking the places where Eskimo *topay*'s had stood. Several stone fireplaces still held fresh ashes. Piled carefully under rocks near the camp were boxes and bales covered in skins. Peetyuk explained that these were caches containing the winter gear of several families of Eskimos.

"Now we almost there," he said jubilantly.

Jamie had a thoughtful look on his face. "Almost *where?*" he asked. "We don't have any idea where the mouth of Big River is on Hudson Bay. Your people never followed the river all the way to its mouth on their winter journeys, Pete. They used to branch off between Edehon and the sea and go across country. We're strictly on our own."

"We know *something* about it, Jamie," Awasin said. "We know the river mouth is north of Churchill. All we must do is turn south along the seacoast."

Jamie snorted. "What an optimist! *All* we have to do is turn south! You don't know the sea, Awasin. Remember that big Eskimo canoe? I tell you *it* wasn't any too big for going on the open sea. I hate to think what will happen to these cockleshells."

Angeline poured them all a mug of tea — almost the last they had. "Why do you worry?" she asked brightly. "We have come many, many miles through this land and we are still alive and healthy. Nothing will happen to us now. With three good men and me we will be fine."

They had not gone more than ten miles the next morning when they shot out into a small triangular-shaped lake. On its northern edge, they saw another sea-going canoe pulled up on shore with a *topay* standing beside it. A wisp of smoke from a small fire showed them that this time they had found living people.

As they paddled toward the camp they were gripped with nervousness. It was rather like stage-fright. It had been so long since they had seen strangers that the prospect of an encounter with an alien people made them feel ill at ease.

They approached so cautiously and quietly that they were within a few yards of shore before they were noticed.

Then an old Eskimo man with a few scraggly black whiskers at his chin came out of the tent, glanced at them, started visibly, and ducked quickly back into the tent. A moment later he again emerged, accompanied by an old woman and two well-grown boys. All four stood and stared dubiously at the strangers, who stared back as silently.

The impasse might have lasted a long time had not Angeline dipped her paddle to drive the canoe shoreward and called out a musical greeting in Cree.

The boys came out of their trance.

"That no good, Angeline. They not understand. I speak."

Peetyuk called out something in his own tongue. The air of silent wariness on the part of the four people ashore seemed to dissipate. The old man shouted something in return and in a moment he and Peetyuk were engaged in a voluble conversation.

At length Peetyuk paused.

"It all right. They good people. We go shore now."

As the canoes were being hauled up on the beach he explained further. "We scare these people. They never hear of anyone come down Big River with canoe in all time Eskimo live here. They not know what we are. But okay now. They understand me pretty good, even though don't talk quite same as my people. They glad have visitors. We go up their tent."

The Sea People, who called themselves Dhaeomiut, proved to be as hospitable and friendly as Eskimos everywhere. The old man, his wife and their two grandsons were part of a family of twelve people. The rest of the family had gone out to the coast three weeks earlier to set up a sealing camp and to trade their fox furs to a white man who, so the old fellow said, lived at the mouth of Big River. The old couple and the two boys had remained behind to net and dry arctic char, a pink-fleshed salmonlike fish.

While the old lady scampered about preparing a huge iron kettleful of char to make a feast, the travelers sat inside the tent talking to the old man and the two wild-looking youths. The news that a white man was living at the mouth of the river was greeted with great excitement.

"Ask him what the fellow's name is, Pete. Find out is he a Hudson Bay Company trader, or what?"

"He say not Hudson Bay man. He say wintertime this man go trapping fox. Spring do a little trading with Sea People. Summertime take big boat and go Iglu-ujaruk — Stone House — what we call Churchill."

"A free trader! Listen, Pete! When does he go to Churchill? Has he gone yet?"

Once more Peetyuk addressed himself to the old man.

"He say not know. Maybe gone, maybe not. Say if we hurry quick, maybe catch. He say Big River split up near mouth. Have many, many channels. Only one take to *kablunak* — white man — house."

"Ask him if he will show us the way," Awasin interjected.

"He not can go himself," Peetyuk replied after posing the question. "But he say one his grandson maybe go with us. Old man, he got no tobacco. Very hungry for tobacco.

Grandson can go and bring back tobacco for old man. He say go tomorrow morning. Now must have big feed and we tell about where we come from."

Despite their anxiety to meet the unknown white man before he left for Churchill, the travelers realized that they would have to curb their impatience. They made the best of the long day that followed. They stuffed themselves on fresh char and on smoked deer-tongues. Curious as pups, they prowled around the camp accompanied by the two Eskimo youths, whose names were Paijak and Mikki-luk. They examined a stone fish weir where the char were diverted into a backwater on their migratory journey up-stream to spawn. And they watched with admiration as Paijak and Mikkiluk demonstrated how they caught the char with long fish spears, triple-tipped like the trident that Neptune is supposed to carry.

That evening they sat for many hours in the tent while the old man talked to Peetyuk. The Meewasins and Jamie were somewhat bored, but Peetyuk and the Eskimos had a fine time of it. This was the first meeting between Ihalmiut and Dhaeomiut in several decades, and there was a great deal to tell on both sides. When Jamie, Awasin and Ange-line went wearily off to sleep, Peetyuk and the Sea People were still hard at it.

CHAPTER 22

Joshua Fudge

Eᴀʀʟʏ ᴛʜᴇ ɴᴇxᴛ ᴍᴏʀɴɪɴɢ ᴛʜᴇ travelers said good-by to the hospitable old couple and again took to the river. Jamie switched over to Awasin's canoe and Angeline now sat amidships. Peetyuk led the way in the other canoe with the young Eskimo, Mikkiluk, paddling bow and acting as pilot.

Under his leadership they had no difficulty negotiating the rapids they encountered during the next few hours. Towards noon Mikkiluk led the way to shore for a brew-up. When the boys and Angeline climbed the steep dike of boulders which formed the riverbank, they found themselves looking out over an infinite expanse of gray waters.

"*Dhaeo!*" Mikkiluk said proudly.

It was indeed the sea — for Hudson Bay is an ocean unto itself measuring over eight hundred miles from north to south and more than four hundred miles in breadth. The sight of that heaving immensity of endless waters had a profound effect upon Peetyuk and the two Meewasins, none of whom had ever seen salt water before.

"*Ai-ya!* He too big for me," Peetyuk exclaimed.

"It would be bad to be out there in a storm," Awasin agreed. "Now I know what you meant, Jamie. It is no place for canoes like ours."

"Maybe we won't need the canoes — if we're lucky. If he hasn't gone yet we may be able to hitch a ride with the free trader. That is, if he's any sort of a half-decent fellow."

They were not long in finding out what sort of fellow he was.

Big River now began to split up into channels that grew in number as they decreased in size. The voyagers were entering the tidal estuary which spreads out over dozens of square miles forming an almost impenetrable maze of channels and low, barren islets. Had it not been for Mikkiluk they might have searched for days before they found the trader's cabin. But Mikkiluk guided them unerringly from channel to channel until they rounded a final bend.

There, on a slight promontory, was an Eskimo camp in the process of being broken up. Mikkiluk yelled and waved and the canoes touched shore.

The goodbyes were quick. Jamie and the others were impatient, and as Mikkiluk pointed from the shore they turned and paddled away from him.

They hardly bothered to wave, for ahead of them on the flat and barren foreshore of Hudson Bay stood a large wooden house. But even more exciting was the sight of a sailing vessel anchored in a lagoon.

Although there was no sign of anyone moving on the

boat, Jamie was so fearful of losing a ride that he risked a swim by standing up in the canoe and announcing their arrival by yelling at the top of his voice.

His shout was answered by a chorus of yelps and howls from a dozen dogs tethered near the cabin. Then the door opened and a big, bald-headed man appeared, his face covered with shaving lather.

The man stood as if transfixed, staring at the approaching canoes. Then he rushed inside, appearing a moment later with a pair of binoculars. He continued to stare through these until the canoes had landed. Not a word did he say, nor did he acknowledge the arrival of visitors by the slightest gesture.

"He does not *seem* too friendly," Awasin said anxiously as they hauled the canoes up above the tide level.

The big man lowered his glasses and stood immobile as the four travelers hesitantly approached him. They noted the bulging muscles of his bare arms, and the hard glare of his blue eyes peering at them over the beard of lather. When he finally spoke he transfixed his visitors, for he had a voice like the bellow of a moose.

"Where in the blank-blank-blank did *you* come from? And who in the blankety-blank *are* ye anyhow?"

Peetyuk and Awasin were tongue-tied, and even Jamie had trouble finding his voice.

"From the Kazon River, sir," he stuttered. "From Thanout Lake, I mean."

"Make up your blinking mind," the big man shouted (for shouting was his normal way of talking). "I guess you're a bunch of whopping liars anyway. Nobody *ever* canoed from Thanout Lake down Big River."

"*We* did, sir, honestly," Jamie said. "I'm Jamie Macnair."

"Macnair? Macnair? No relation to Angus Macnair, be ye?"

"I'm his nephew, sir. These two, they're the son and daughter of Mr. Meewasin, the chief of the Crees at Thanout. And this is Peetyuk Anderson — his dad was a trapper on the Barrens."

"Anderson too, eh? Why blank me, this is like old home week. Well, what are you standin' there for? Come in! Come in!" And he stood aside so they could enter his home.

Since there were no trees anywhere near the mouth of Big River, the house had been built of planed timber brought by schooner from Churchill. It had four rooms, many windows, three stoves, and was filled with shiny mail-order furniture. A glittering radio blared away from the kitchen table, and small light bulbs on the ceiling showed that the owner had a generating plant to make his own electricity.

The big man suddenly remembered his lathered face. With a muffled apology he grabbed a towel and wiped off the lather. Then he began to bustle about at a great rate, heaping coal on the kitchen range and slapping dishes on the table.

"Wherever ye belong, ye look nigh starved. You needs a scoff! What'll it be? Bacon and eggs and seal steaks suit ye?"

The travelers could only nod their heads dumbly, for they were overwhelmed by the change in their situation. Only a few hours ago they had been nomads living in a lonely, empty land. Now they were in the lap of such luxury as Peetyuk and the Meewasins had never known, and such as Jamie had not seen for several years. It was enough to strike them all dumb.

"Got no tongues in yere heads?" the big man shouted. "I'm Joshua Fudge. Belong to Newfoundland, I do. Been in this blank-blank country for thirty years now. Don't know why I stays. Knew Frank Anderson pretty good a long spell back. Told him he was a damn fool to go into the Barrens. He wouldn't listen. So you're his son, eh? Got his hair, anyway. And Angus Macnair. The old so-and-so's still living, is he? Trapped three seasons with him on the Mackenzie. You're his nephew? Pretty puny one, if you asks me. Now here's your grub. Scoff it down, me sons. Don't mind me. I talks a lot. But then I ain't had nobody but Eskimos to talk to for a year. Kind of get bottled up inside me, ye might say. . . ."

Once started, Josh apparently could not stop talking. But as he roared on, the visitors dug into the welcome meal and began to feel a little more at home. By the time they had finished they had grown used to the bellowing, and had begun to like their host. When breakfast, or lunch, or whatever one would call it, was over, Josh poured pint mugs of coffee for all hands and herded them into the next room. This was a spacious living room equipped with easy chairs and with masses of books and magazines piled against the walls.

"Sit ye down, me sons. Sorry, missy! Don't mind what I calls you. It's only the way I has of talkin'. We don't see many ladies in these parts, not counting Eskimo ladies. Sorry to you, Peter, or whatever your name is. I meant no harm to the Eskimos. They're the finest friends I got. Might say the only friends. Now, then, what the devil is all this about coming down Big River? Where did you *really* come from, and how?"

Josh relapsed into temporary silence as Jamie told the story of the trip through the Barrens. The big man grew more and more interested, leaning forward in his chair until he was almost falling off the edge of it. "You don't say?" he would bellow at intervals, but he let Jamie continue until the tale was told.

"So that's the way of it? Well, me sons, ye came to the right place. Macnair in trouble? And the Mounties after you younkers? Ha! We'll see about all that. And them Viking things? I'd like to cast me eyes on them if I might. Now then, you younkers. I figured on sailing for Churchill day after tomorrow. That good enough for ye? We'll make the run in two days, weather willing. Once we makes Churchill I'll get on the telegraph. We'll find out about Angus right smart — that we will. And if needs be I'll go along of ye to The Pas. Time I had a holiday in the bright lights anyway. By the living blank-blank-blank there ain't nobody will lay a hand on ye if Josh Fudge is standing nigh!"

He paused as he saw that he was losing his audience. The excitement of their overwhelming welcome at Josh Fudge's, together with the warmth of the room and the relief of knowing that their lonely voyage was at an end, had combined to render the travelers unbearably sleepy. Josh understood.

"Best haul down the sails for now, I reckons. Time for the watch below. Off with the lot of ye. There's two bedrooms. Yes, and even sheets on one of the beds. That'll be for the young lady. The rest of ye can bunk together. Git, now! I'll see to yere gear."

The strain of the voyage down Big River was at an end, and the uncertainty about how they would get to Churchill was resolved. The boys and Angeline now had nothing to do but take things easy, eat, sleep, and satisfy their curiosity about their host.

Josh was a magnificent cook. The table was always heaped with fresh bread, doughnuts, great roasts of meat, potatoes, apple pies, stewed fruit and cookies. He never stopped talking, and he was full of yarns about his own experiences.

He told them how he had first come north as an apprentice with the Hudson Bay Company, but had tired of hard work for little pay and had gone off trapping on his own. During his thirty years in the arctic he had wandered all the way from Baffin Island to Alaska, amassing a not inconsiderable fortune in the process. Ten years earlier he had decided to settle down at the mouth of Big River, and here he had built his elaborate house which was now a legend for comfort all through the north. He did not work too hard any more, contenting himself with running a few traplines for white fox on the lower reaches of Big

River. More or less by accident he had also become the trader for the Big River Eskimos, who found it difficult to make the long journey south to Churchill even in their big sea-going canoes. So Josh took their furs and supplied them with their needs, but he ran the trading business almost at cost — making little or no profit on it. It was a service which he rendered to the Eskimos. In the summer months he and some of his particular friends amongst the Eskimo men took his schooner, the *Arctica*, on exploring and hunting voyages along the coasts of Hudson Bay. The previous year they had been as far north as Southampton Island, hunting walrus for winter dog food.

His stories fascinated all his visitors, but Peetyuk was particularly interested. The first sight of the sea seemed to have affected him like a fever. He could not hear enough about it and he was constantly pestering Josh to tell him more.

The day after their arrival Josh took the young people out to see his vessel. She was a fifty-foot Newfoundland schooner. In addition to her sails she was fitted with a powerful diesel engine. She had been specially built for ice navigation and was double-sheathed with iron-hard greenheart planking. She had a roomy main cabin with a good galley in it, a saloon table and bunks for four, and up in her bows was a forepeak cabin with four more bunks.

The boys climbed into every nook and corner of her.

"What a way to travel!" Jamie exclaimed as he sat with the others drinking coffee in the schooner's cabin. "No more canoes, no more rain, no more being wind-bound, no more leaky tents . . ."

"No more go down big rapids . . ." Peetyuk added.

"No more mosquitoes either," said Angeline.

Josh Fudge's blue eyes gleamed as he listened to their enthusiastic remarks.

"Tell you what," he boomed. "I'll sign the lot of ye on for a voyage. Why don't you come along of me this summer? We'll make a trip to Boothia — that's where the magnetic pole's supposed to be. Might bring it back for a souvenir."

"Thanks a lot, Mr. Fudge — Josh," Jamie replied. "I guess we'd all give our right arms to go with you. But we have to get on south. We have to sell the Viking things we found, and look after my uncle, and try and do something for the inland Eskimos."

CHAPTER 23

Journey's End

IMMEDIATELY AFTER BREAKFAST all hands went to work loading Josh's furs and the youngsters' kit and canoes aboard the *Arctica*. Josh checked over the vessel's gear and tested the engine. By noon she was ready to sail.

It was a fine day with a brisk breeze off the land — a "quartering breeze," as Josh called it. Helped by the boys, who took readily to their new roles as deckhands, Josh soon had the sails set, the anchor hauled home, and the schooner's head pointed out to sea.

She stood straight out from the land until the low-lying coastal plains had sunk out of sight behind them. Josh explained that it was necessary to stay well offshore because the coast to the southward was dangerously shoal. But the experience of leaving the land behind and finding themselves surrounded by a gray void of ocean unnerved Peetyuk.

"What we do if sink?" Peetyuk asked his friends anxiously.

"Whistle up a whale and get a ride ashore," Jamie answered cheerfully. "Don't worry, we won't sink. And if we did we still have our canoes, and there's a big dory for a lifeboat."

The remark about whales must have been prophetic. As Josh altered course to run southward, Awasin, who was standing near the bow, let out a warning shout. Directly ahead of the vessel a score of small waterspouts broke the surface and a moment later a number of great, white gleaming bodies arched into view.

"Beluga — white whales," Josh explained. "The bay's full of they."

In their curiosity about the whales Peetyuk and the Meewasins forgot to be nervous, and within a few hours they had settled down to life afloat. They were full of questions and Josh was kept busy explaining how to steer a course, how to keep the sails properly set, and many other nautical matters.

The wind held steady off the land so there was no sea or swell to set the youngsters' stomachs heaving. Because there was no real darkness Josh kept the vessel driving south all through the night. Towards evening of the following day Awasin, who had been sent up the weather shrouds at Josh's order to act as lookout, spotted the distant loom of the gigantic concrete grain elevator at Churchill — the end of the railroad and the point from which prairie wheat is shipped to Europe in summertime over the short arctic route.

As the *Arctica* came around and headed into the mouth of the Churchill River, Josh started the engine and helped the boys take down the sail. They came chugging in past the ruins of ancient Fort Prince of Wales, which gives

Churchill its Eskimo name of Stone House, and pulled alongside the Government dock.

Peetyuk and the Meewasins stared bug-eyed at the huge structure of the elevator, towering several hundred feet into the air. They were equally amazed by the size of two ocean-going freighters loading at the long wharf, and by the roar and rattle of a freight train, laden with wheat, which was just pulling in to the dockside terminal at the end of its seven-hundred-mile run north from Winnipeg.

They were not allowed to stand and stare for long. Once the lines were made fast, Josh ordered everyone below.

"I wants all of ye to stay aboard, and keep out of sight," he told them. "They's a big Mountie detachment here. I'll go ashore and mosey about. I knows everybody in Churchill and everybody knows me. When I finds out if the Mounties is looking for you I'll be back. Light up the galley fire and get yourselves a scoff; but mind now, keep down below!"

Jamie found himself left with the chore of getting supper. Peetyuk, Angeline and Awasin had their faces glued to the cabin portholes examining this — the first real town they had ever seen. Jamie was glad of a job to do, for he was now extremely nervous about the police.

Several hours went by before the youngsters heard the tramp of heavy boots on deck. Tensely they eyed the companion ladder and when Josh descended into view they were much relieved. But they tensed again when they saw that he was accompanied by a stranger.

The newcomer was clean-shaven and smartly dressed in city clothes.

"This here's a perfessor fellow from the south," Josh said by way of introduction. "I run into Old Windy Jones and he tole me this here fellow was digging in the ruins at Fort Prince of Wales. I figured he'd know about them old things you got, so I tracked him down to his hotel. And here he is."

The stranger smiled. "My name is Armstrong," he said in a pleasant voice. "Actually I'm an archaeologist with the Dominion Museum in Ottawa. We're doing research on the old fort. My own field of study is the early colonial period but it just happens that I know something about Norse culture, too. Mr. Fudge tells me you have some things you think might be Norse?"

"Maybe we have," Jamie replied cautiously, for he was afraid of saying too much to the wrong person.

"I assure you it's quite safe to tell me about it. Whatever you've got is yours by right of finding it. Nobody can take it away from you. And perhaps I might be of some help by giving an opinion on your finds."

Jamie glanced at Peetyuk and Awasin, and when they nodded their heads he got to his feet, rummaged under one of the bunks, and pulled out the carefully wrapped packages. Placing them on the saloon table he cut the lashings and drew back the deerskin coverings.

The archaeologist bent over the table and minutely examined the sword and helmet. He whistled lightly between his teeth.

"These *seem to* be the real thing, boys," he told them. "I didn't really believe it when Mr. Fudge told me what you thought you'd found. But this is almost certainly a twelfth or thirteenth century Scandinavian sword and helmet. What's in the soapstone box?"

"We're not sure, sir," Jamie replied, his caution forgotten. "We didn't want to mess up the stuff that's in it. We thought we'd better leave it alone till some expert could look it over."

Armstrong nodded his head approvingly. "Very wise. But I see a Nordic armlet there — looks like a gold one too."

"That belong Koonar. All stuff belong Koonar one time," Peetyuk said.

Armstrong's eyebrows shot up. "How do you know the name of the man? I think you'd best tell me the whole story of your find."

He sat on a bunk and listened intently as Jamie, assisted now and again by one of the others, told the story, beginning with the finding of the stone tomb the previous summer. By the time Jamie had finished the archaeologist had become extremely excited. He got to his feet and began pacing the length of the cabin.

"I don't want to say too much until we've checked all the facts. There's that lead tablet you have at your cabin, for instance. That will have to be examined by qualified runologists. But I'll go out on a limb partway — I think you young people *may* have made one of the most valuable and important historical finds of the century.

"Now we'd better decide how to proceed from here. These relics are far too valuable to be left lying around. I think you should place them in the hands of the police for safekeeping. I'll radio my colleagues in Ottawa this very night. . . . What's the matter? Did I say something wrong?" He cast a puzzled glance at Jamie, who now appeared very nervous and ill at ease and was desperately trying to catch Josh's eye.

"I reckon I know the trouble, Perfessor. But you got nothing to worry about, Jamie. I had a yarn with one of the corporals at the detachment. Old chum of mine. He says he never heard tell of you. There's no 'wanted' poster out on you. What's more, he says since you're nearly sixteen there likely never was no idea of putting you into an orphan asylum. He figures they just wanted to make sure you didn't starve up in the woods alone. Looks like you run halfway across the arctic all for nothing. Running from shadows, you might say." He chuckled at the expression of relief mixed with embarrassment on Jamie's face.

"There's more news for you. I wired the hospital at The Pas. Got an answer back right off. Angus Macnair's been convalescent for pretty near a month, and he's due for discharge anytime. So I sends a wire off to him, telling the old buffalo to meet us at Hudson Bay Junction Tuesday next, when the weekly train goes south."

The archaeologist looked baffled as the three boys and Angeline leaped to their feet shouting with delight, and clamoring for more details.

"Whoa there!" Josh bellowed. "Steady down! The perfessor here'll think you're 'bushed.' Where's your manners, eh? Missy Angeline, put on a pot of coffee for the man. Now then, Jamie, I figures you can trust the perfessor here. Windy Jones reckons he's okay, and Windy don't make no mistakes. You'd best do what he says."

"Thank you, Mr. Fudge. You can certainly trust me, boys — and you too, young lady. We'll get a receipt from the police for the relics. If I get the reception I expect from my radio message to Ottawa, I'll come south with you myself and we'll arrange to have some museum specialists from Ottawa and Toronto meet us in Winnipeg. Perhaps you would agree to going on as far as Winnipeg? I can guarantee that the National Museum will pay all your expenses for the journey."

A week later when the train left Churchill for the long run south it carried four excited youngsters, all of them togged out at Josh's expense in brand-new "store clothing." The boys felt somewhat stiff and peculiar in their new gear, but Angeline was delighted with a smart new dress which made her feel as pretty as she looked — and that was pretty enough to draw a good many admiring glances from other male passengers, and to make Peetyuk growl a little with barely suppressed jealousy.

This was the first train ride Awasin, Angeline and Peetyuk had ever taken and they found it fascinating. Crowded on the rear platform they watched the rails slip away behind them as the clattering train swung away from the gray waters of Hudson Bay and plunged into the stunted spruce forests. And although a train trip was no novelty for Jamie he was just as excited as were the others, for a telegram had arrived shortly before their departure telling him that Angus Macnair would join the party at Hudson Bay Junction. It had been decided that they would all go on to Winnipeg together and enjoy a holiday in that prairie city while the Viking relics were being examined by the experts.

Josh Fudge joined them on the open platform and after a moment he drew their attention to the pale evening sky where a black and straggling "V" of Canada geese also pointed southward.

"The Big River people claims them geese carries summer with them when they takes to wing," he told his young companions. "And in the spring, they brings it back. Maybe when they pitches at Big River next year you younkers'll come along with they; and we can make that voyage to the nor'west we talked about . . . but that's for later on. Right now let's go and see what kind o' grub they gives a feller on this here 'muskeg express.' . . ."